A WILLIE SPEIGHT FILM

THE HOLLOWAY STORY

WILLIE SPEIGHT

authorHOUSE®

AuthorHouse™
1663 Liberty Drive
Bloomington, IN 47403
www.authorhouse.com
Phone: 1-800-839-8640

First published by AuthorHouse 6/7/2010

ISBN: 978-1-4520-3618-2 (e)
ISBN: 978-1-4520-3617-5 (sc)

Printed in the United States of America
Bloomington, Indiana

This book is printed on acid-free paper.

INTRODUCTION

INSPIRED BY A TRUE STORY

PLACE: SUMTER COUNTY HIGH SCHOOL

POPULATION: 2,692

LOCATION: YORK, ALABAMA

YEAR: 1987

IN THE SPRING OF 1987 PATRICIA HANNAH, A FELLOW STUDENT AT SUMTER COUNTY HIGH SCHOOL, WAS LEAVING A HIGH SCHOOL DANCE AROUND 1AM. SHE WAS ABDUCTED AND KILLED. HER BODY WAS DISCOVERED ONE WEEK LATER BY AN EMPLOYEE OF ALABAMA POWER COMPANY.

CHAPTER 1

"EXCUSE ME DR. GOLDMAN, YOUR SON, DR. ANDERSON GOLDMAN, IS ON LINE TWO," SAYS DR. GOLDMAN'S SECRETARY.

"SON", SAYS DR. GOLDMAN.

"SHE'S DYING DAD."

"WHAT'S WRONG?"

"IT'S HER HEART DAD!"

"TRY TO REMAIN CALM SON. I'M THE HEART SPECIALIST. LET'S FIGURE THIS OUT NOW! WHAT'S WRONG WITH HER HEART?"

"IT DOESN'T LOOK GOOD! HER HEART IS FAILING BECAUSE OF SOME VIRUS THAT SHE HAD!"

"IS SHE ON THE DONOR'S LIST?"

"NO. THERE'RE NO DONOR HEARTS AVAILABLE FOR HER, DAD! HOW CAN WE GET AN ORGAN, IF THERE'RE NONE AVAILABLE?"

"AS YOU WELL KNOW, THERE'S A WAY AROUND ANYTHING! LET ME MAKE A CALL TO A CLOSE FRIEND OF MINE. I'LL GET YOU A HEART SON. HANG IN THERE. I'LL GET YOU A HEART."

"HURRY DAD! PLEASE HURRY!"

DR. GOLDMAN CALLS HIS FRIEND THE SHERIFF WHO CAN HELP HIM GET WHAT HE NEEDS TO SAVE HIS DAUGHTER-IN-LAW'S LIFE. HIS SON SOUNDED DESPERATE AND HE WILL HELP HIM IN ANY WAY HE CAN.

"SHERIFF PRICE'S OFFICE," SAYS LOCAL OPERATOR.

"SHERIFF PRICE PLEASE", SAYS DR. GOLDMAN.

"HE'S IN A MEETING. CAN I HELP YOU WITH SOMETHING"?, ASKS THE OPERATOR.

"WALK INTO HIS MEETING AND TELL HIM DR. GOLDMAN IS ON THE PHONE".

"I'M SORRY DR. GOLDMAN, I'M NOT ALLOWED TO DO THAT!"

"DAMN IT! DO WHAT I SAY!" YELLED DR. GOLDMAN.

THE OPERATOR CONNECTS THE CALL TO SHERIFF PRICE. "SHERIFF PRICE SPEAKING".

"MEET ME IN AN HOUR", SAYS DR. GOLDMAN.

"WHERE?", ASKS THE SHERRIFF.

"IN MY OFFICE", ANSWERS DR. GOLDMAN.

"CONCERNING"?, ASKS THE SHERIFF.

"A HEART, IT'S FOR MY DAUGHTER IN LAW".

CHAPTER 2

SUMTER COUNTY HIGH SCHOOL

"CHEESE, GIVE ME THIS BROOM. IT'S LUNCH TIME. TAKE A BREAK," SAYS SIERRA, PLAYFULLY CALLING SHELTON BY THE NAME THAT HE IS KNOWN BY IN THE COMMUNITY.

"LUNCH, I'M ON THE CLOCK. MY NEXT LUNCH BREAK IS AT 3", STUTTERS SHELTON. SHELTON HAS HAD A SPEECH IMPEDIMENT SINCE HE WAS A CHILD. IT WOULD BECOME WORSE WHEN HE BECAME NERVOUS.

"SCHOOL'S OUT AT 3."

"I KNOW".

"WHEN DO YOU EAT LUNCH?" ASKS SIERRA.

"WHEN I GET TO MILLER CONSTRUCTION"

SURPRISED, SIERRA REPEATS, "MILLER CONSTRUCTION"?

"THAT'S MY SECOND JOB".

"YOU'RE TRULY A DEDICATED MAN SHELTON. WE NEED MORE MEN LIKE YOU AROUND."

"THANKS. I CAN'T BELIEVE A PRETTY LADY LIKE YOU WOULD TAKE TIME TO SPEAK TO SOMEBODY LIKE ME. I'M JUST A JANITOR."

"SHELTON, YOU'RE MORE THAN A JANITOR. THIS IS YOUR SCHOOL TOO. YOU ATTEND CLASSES JUST LIKE ME."

"YEAH, I KNOW!"

"YOU THINK I'M PRETTY SHELTON?"

SHELTON STUTTERS AND REPLIES, "YES! SMART AND FINE TOO!"

"OOH! YOU'RE SO SWEET! I WISH MY BOYFRIEND WOULD SAY THOSE THINGS TO ME."

SHELTON BECOMES EXCITED AND SAYS, "I'LL BE YOUR BOYFRIEND!"

"GOODBYE SHELTON", SIERRA SAYS AS SHE WALKS AWAY.

CHAPTER 3

**DR. GOLDMAN IS SITTING IN HIS OFFICE TALK-
ING TO THE SHERIFF.**

"HAVE YOU THOUGHT ABOUT THIS", INQUIRES
THE SHERIFF.

"THERE'S NOTHING TO THINK ABOUT. WE
NEED A FEMALE THAT'S IN GREAT PHYSICAL
SHAPE", REPLIES DR. GOLDMAN.

"A YOUNG PERSON, I'M THINKING WE CAN
WAIT ON A DONOR".

"I DON'T HAVE TIME TO WAIT! I'M IN A CRISIS.
MY DAUGHTER IN LAW IS DYING. SHE NEEDS A
HEART, AND SHE NEEDS IT FAST!"

"I DON'T KNOW. I HAVE TO THINK ABOUT
THIS".

DR. GOLDMAN REACHES OVER THE DESK AND
GRABS THE SHERIFF BY HIS SHIRT. "YOU LISTEN

TO ME AND YOU LISTEN GOOD! I MADE YOU! HOW IN THE HELL DO YOU THINK YOU BECAME THE SHERRIFF AROUND HERE? IN CASE YOU FORGOT, I RIGGED THE ELECTION! AND A LOT OF PEOPLE ARE STILL SUSPICIOUS ABOUT THAT!"

"YOU'RE RIGHT. I GUESS I DIDN'T THINK ABOUT THAT", THE SHERIFF SAYS WHILE RELEASING HIS SHIRT.

"I'M GLAD YOU SEE THINGS MY WAY. HERE'S THE PLAN. AS YOU KNOW, I'M AN EX ORGAN BROKER WHO TRAFFICKED ORGANS. MY SON AND I WILL ABDUCT AN INNOCENT BLACK FEMALE AND PERFORM THE SURGERY TO REMOVE HER ORGANS. YOU FIND THE PERSON TO PLANT THE CRIME SCENE EVIDENCE ON. I'LL PAY OFF THE JUDGE, THE MAYOR, THE DISTRICT ATTORNEY OR WHOEVER MAY GET IN OUR WAY!"

"I'M AFRAID IT'S NOT THAT EASY. WHAT IF THE FAMILY HAS MONEY TO BRING IN A BIG SHOT ATTORNEY? TIMES HAVE CHANGED", EXPLAINS THE SHERIFF.

"OUR GOOD OLD FRIEND JUDGE LEVY WILL REJECT ANY WITNESSES TESTIFING ON THE DE-

FENDANT'S BEHALF. WE NEED TO FIND JUST
THE RIGHT PERSON WHO CAN BE BLAMED".

"WE LIVE IN YORK, ALABAMA. POPULATION
2600 PEOPLE WITH ONE PUBLIC SCHOOL! DO
YOU KNOW HOW HARD IT IS TO FIND SUCH A
PERSON? HELL, EVERYONE HERE KNOW EACH
OTHER"!

"I'LL FIGURE IT OUT. IT'S BEEN A LONG TIME
SINCE I'VE HAD TO DO THIS, BUT I CAN GET IT
DONE"!

"I DON'T SEE HOW YOU ARE GOING TO PULL
THIS OFF."

DR. GOLDDMAN YELLS, "ME! THAT'S WHAT I'M
PAYING YOU TO DO"!

THE SHERIFF TURNS HIS BACK AND PREPARES
TO WALK OUT THE ROOM. "AND IF ANYTHING
GOES WRONG, WE'D ALL BETTER BE PREPARED
TO LEAVE TOWN!"

"I'LL BE READY", SAYS DR. GOLDMAN.

NANCY, DR. GOLDMAN'S LONG TIME SECRE-
TARY INTERRUPTS, "DR. GOLDMAN, YOU HAVE
A CALL ON LINE 4".

"NANCY WOULD YOU PLEASE COME INTO MY OFFICE"?, ASKS DR. GOLDMAN.

WHILE DR. GOLDMAN ANSWERS THE CALL, NANCY WALKS INTO THE ROOM. "DR.GOLD-MAN SPEAKING".

"I HAVE AN APPOINTMENT AT 1 P.M. TODAY, BUT I CAN'T MAKE IT UNTIL 2", SAYS JUDY.

"2 O'CLOCK WILL BE FINE".

"YES. DR. GOLDMAN?", SAYS NANCY WHO HAS BEEN WAITING IN DR. GOLDMAN'S OFFICE.

"DON'T SCHEDULE ANY MORE PATIENTS AFTER MY LAST. I NEED TO LEAVE ON TIME TODAY."

CHAPTER 4

IT'S THE BEGINNING OF THE SCHOOL DAY FOR THE STUDENTS AT SUMTER COUNTY. THE SCHOOL BELL RINGS. STUDENTS WALK OUT OF THE CLASSROOM.

BEFORE THE STUDENTS RUN OUT OF CLASS, MRS. LITTLE REMINDS THE CLASS OF THE WRITTEN EXAM TOMORROW. WAVING HER HANDS, MRS. LITTLE SHOUTS, "SHELTON"!

STUTTERING, SHELTON ANSWERS "YES, YES MRS. LITTLE?"

"I HOPE YOU WON'T FORGET YOUR CLASS SCHEDULE THIS YEAR", MRS. LITTLE SAYS AS SHE PASSES SHELTON HIS CLASS SCHEDULE AND IQ SCORE.

SHELTON LOOKS AT THE PAPER AND ASKS, "WHAT'S THIS?"

"YOUR CLASS SCHEDULE AND YOUR IQ SCORE". MRS. LITTLE CRIES AS SHE SAYS, "SHELTON, YOUR IQ IS 40".

"40?,"SO THAT'S GOOD, HUH?"

"NO SON, IT'S NOT GOOD. YOU ARE IN THE 12TH GRADE, AND YOUR IQ SCORE IS THAT OF A THIRD GRADER".

"MAYBE I SHOULD GIVE UP ON MY LIFE. I MEAN, I'M JUST A HIGH SCHOOL JANITOR. I'LL NEVER AMOUNT TO ANYTHING. SHELTON SAYS STUTTERING. "I'M 20 YEARS OLD. I BEEN IN THE 12TH GRADE FOR TWO YEARS NOW."

MRS. LITTLE SHAKES HER HEAD AND ASKS, "WHERE ARE YOUR PARENTS?"

"MY MOM IS HOME WAITING ON HER FOOD STAMPS TO COME IN THE MAIL ON THE 3RD DAY OF EVERY MONTH. I DON'T REMEMBER MY FATHER. HE DIED WHEN I WAS A LITTLE BOY."

"DO YOU HAVE BROTHERS AND SISTERS?"

"I'M THE OLDEST OF FIVE CHILDREN. MY BABY SISTER LIVES WITH MY MOM! SHE HELPS ME WITH MY HOMEWORK."

"HOW OLD IS SHE?"

"SIX! I'M SORRY MRS. LITTLE, I HAVE TO GO TO MY SECOND JOB."

CHAPTER 5

"HI HONEY, WHERE'S DAVID, ASKS DR. GOLDMAN.

DR. GOLDMAN'S WIFE ISABELLA POINTS UPSTAIRS.

DAVID GOLDMAN'S ROOM IS SURROUNDED WITH BLACK DOLLS. HE IS GETTING HIGH ON COCAINE, LOOKING OUT THE WINDOW AT YOUNG HIGH SCHOOL GIRLS WALKING THE SIDEWALK AFTER SCHOOL. HE MAKES EYES CONTACT WITH PATRICIA HANNAH WALKING WHO IS WALKING WITH HER FRIENDS.

"YOU BETTER KEEP GOING BEFORE I GRAB YOU!" SCREAMS DAVID.

DR. GOLDMAN WALKS INTO HIS SON'S ROOM.

AFTER SNIFFING COCAINE, SECONDS LATER HE'S SMOKING WEED. HIS FINGERS ARE BLACK. "I LOVE BLACK GIRLS!"

"SON, WHAT DO BLACK GIRLS HAVE THAT WHITE GIRLS DON'T?" ASKS DR. GOLDMAN.

STILL SNIFFING COCAINE, DAVID REPLIES, "ARE YOU KIDDING ME? THEIR SWEET SCENT AND THEIR FRAGANCE. BLACK GIRLS COME IN ALL SHAPES AND SIZES. HE GRABS A BLACK DOLL AND PLAYS WITH HER HAIR. "THEIR BMD IS HIGHER THAN WHITE GIRLS."

DR. GOLDMAN ASKS, "BMD. WHAT'S A BMD?"

"YOU'RE A DOCTOR AND DON'T KNOW WHAT BMD MEANS? HE LAUGHS, "THAT'S FUNNY AS SHIT! BONE MASS DENSITY!"

"THEIR PHYSICAL FEATURES WERE CHISELED BY THEIR AFRICAN ANCESTORS AND BLENDED WITH MIDDLE PASSAGE HERITAGE."

"I DON'T KNOW HOW YOU CAN BE MY SON, WITH YOUR BLACK COCAINE FINGERS, SITTING IN A WINDOW ALL DAY SNIFFING COCAINE AND WATCHING HIGH SCHOOL GIRLS WALKING THE SIDEWALK! YOU SURE DO KNOW A LOT ABOUT BLACK WOMEN!"

"THERE'S A REASON WHY THESE BLACK GIRLS WALK THE SIDEWALK."

"SURE THERE IS. THAT'S THE ONLY WAY THAT THEY CAN GET TO SCHOOL."

"THAT'S NOT THE ONLY REASON, DAD!"

"WHAT'S THE OTHER REASON SON?"

"ED'S FOOD MART. THEY WALK TO THE GAS STATION TO CATCH A RIDE AND HANGOUT".

CHAPTER 6

"HOW WAS SCHOOL TODAY?", ASKS HELEN HANNAH, PATRICIA'S MOTHER.

"BORING", ANSWERS PATRICIA.

"BORING"? REPEATS PATRICIA'S MOTHER.

"MOM, I'M AN A AND B STUDENT. I'M ON A COLLEGE LEVEL".

"I KNOW PATRICIA. I GUESS I SHOULD START GETTING USED TO IT. YOU'LL BE A SENIOR NEXT YEAR. THEN YOU HEAD OFF TO RICHMOND COLLEGE IN TUSCALOOSA. I KNOW! COME TO THE TABLE. DINNER IS READY."

PATRICIA WALKS TO THE DINNER TABLE WITH HER DIARY AND HER BLUE JEANS.

"DO YOU HAVE TO BRING YOUR DIARY TO THE DINNER TABLE EVERY TIME YOU EAT? WHERE

DO YOU THINK YOU'RE GOING WITH THOSE JEANS"?

"MOM, MY DIARY IS MY LIFE. IT'S THERAPEUTIC. IT'S A GREAT WAY FOR ME TO KEEP UP WITH MY THOUGHTS. MY JEANS? I'M WEARING THEM TO THE DANCE TOMORROW NIGHT. THEY ARE MY FAVORITE PAIR. YOU BOUGHT THEM FOR ME ON MY 16TH BIRTHDAY, AND THEY FIT JUST RIGHT".

"ARE YOU STILL PLANNING ON GOING TO THE HIGH SCHOOL DANCE TOMORROW NIGHT? I DON'T WANT THOSE LITTLE MANISH TAIL BOYS AROUND YOU".

"YES MOM. I'M GOING TO DANCE. CARLOS IS THE ONLY BOY THAT WILL BE AROUND ME".

"WHAT TIME WILL THIS DANCE BE OVER"?

"THE GREEK SHOW STARTS AROUND 8 PM".

"A GREEK SHOW? I DIDN'T KNOW ABOUT THAT", INQUIRES PATRICIA'S MOM.

"YES MOM. WE ARE HAVING OUR LAST GREEK SHOW FOR THE YEAR. OUR DANCE SHOULD BE OVER AROUND 12 A.M. FOR THE FIRST TIME IN 16 YEARS, MY DIARY WILL BE WITH ME AT THE GREEK SHOW".

"WHY WOULD YOU TAKE YOUR DIARY TO A GREEK SHOW PATRICIA"?

"I WOULD LIKE FOR SOME OF MY SENIOR FRIENDS TO SIGN MY BOOK, SINCE IT'S THEIR LAST YEAR IN SCHOOL".

"I SEE".

"MOM"?

"YES DARLING"

PATRICIA ASKS IN A SOFT VOICE, "IF ANYTHING EVER HAPPENED TO ME, WOULD YOU MISS ME"?

"PATRICIA! DON'T SAY THAT"!

"REALLY MOM," WOULD YOU MISS ME"?

"YES, I WOULD MISS YOU. SHE PUTS HER HANDS ON HER CHEEKS. YOU DON'T HAVE TO WORRY ABOUT DYING ANYTIME SOON YOUNG LADY! YOU'RE FULL OF LIFE! YOU'RE ONLY 16 YEARS OLD"!

"MOM, YOU KNOW THAT SIDEWALK I TAKE WHEN I WALK TO SCHOOL? THE SIDEWALK EVERYONE TAKES"?

"YES. WHAT ABOUT IT"?

"IT HAD MY NAME IN LIGHTS".

"PATRICIA WHAT ARE YOU TALKING ABOUT"?

"I DREAMED THAT I SAW MY NAME IN LIGHTS BY THE SIDEWALK".

"HONEY THAT WAS JUST A DREAM".

PATRICIA'S VOICE GETS LOUDER. "SOMETHING HAPPENS TO ME ON THAT SIDEWALK MOM! I SAW IT"!

HELEN'S VOICE GETS LOUDER. "PATRICIA STOP IT"!

PATRICIA GETS UP AND RUNS TO HER ROOM, AND HER MOM FOLLOWS. PATRICIA LIES ACROSS HER BED.

"I'M SORRY YOU HAD A BAD DREAM", HELEN SAYS SOFTLY WHILE RUBBING PATRICIA'S HAIR. "MOMMY LOVES YOU". THE TWO HUG.

HELEN GRABS THE DIARY OFF THE DRESSER. "PATRICIA, SINCE IT MAKES YOU SO UPSET, THEN YOU DON'T NEED TO GO ANYWHERE NEAR THAT SIDEWALK! I'LL DROP YOU OFF AT

THE SCHOOL, AND HONEY, LEAVE YOUR DIARY AT HOME".

"OKAY MOM"!

"I ADDED A SECOND PHONE LINE IN MY ROOM", SAYS HELEN. SHE PASSES HER DAUGHTER THE NEW NUMBER. "HERE, PUT THIS NUMBER IN YOUR POCKET".

"WHY DID YOU DO THAT"?

"IT'S A MOM THING".

"I LOVE YOU MOM".

"I LOVE YOU TOO PATRICIA. HAVE FUN TOMOR-ROW AT THE DANCE". SHE TAKES THE DIARY AND PUTS IT ON THE DRESSER. "LEAVE YOUR DIARY ON THIS DRESSER".

"I WILL".

"GOODNIGHT".

"GOODNIGHT MOM".

THE NEXT MORNING HELEN HANNAH WALKS INTO PATRICIA ROOM TO SEE THE DIARY MISSING.

CHAPTER 7

"YOU'LL BE FINE", DR. GOLDMAN SAYS, TALKING
TO HIS PATIENT.

"DR. GOLDMAN, YOUR SON DR. ANDERSON
GOLDMAN IS ON LINE TWO", SAYS NANCY, DR.
GOLDMAN'S SECRETARY.

"NANCY, DID YOU LOOK UP THOSE FILES"?

"I'VE GOT THEM RIGHT HERE", ANSWERS NANCY.

"THREE, WE ONLY HAD THREE FILES OVER THE
PASS 6 MONTHS"?

"NO, WE HAD HUNDREDS OF FILES OVER THE
PAST 6 MONTHS".

"SO, WHERE ARE THE REST OF THEM"?

"THOSE FILES ARE WHITE PATIENTS. YOU SAID
YOU ONLY WANTED BLACK PATIENT FILES. SO
THERE YOU HAVE IT, THREE".

DR. GOLDMAN TAKES THE CALL FROM HIS SON, DR. ANDERSON GOLDMAN.

"HAVE YOU FOUND A DONOR YET"?, ASKS ANDERSON.

"NOT YET SON, I'M STILL WORKING ON IT".

"YOU'RE WORKING ON IT? DAD, I'M RUNNING OUT OF TIME"!

"SON, GIVE ME MORE TIME".

"DAMN IT DADDY! I HAVE 48 HOURS LEFT! MY WIFE IS DYING HOW MUCH TIME DO YOU NEED? IF THIS WAS MOM, YOU WOULD HAVE FOUND A DONOR BY NOW"!

"DON'T EVER DISRESPECT YOUR MOTHER"!

"I'M NOT DISRESPECTING MOM, DAD. I'M LOOK-ING OUT FOR MY WIFE. SHE'S ALL I HAVE"!

"SON, I UNDERSTAND YOU'RE LOOKING OUT FOR YOUR WIFE. ALL I'M ASKING YOU IS FOR MORE TIME. GIVE ME MORE TIME".

"HOW'S DAVID", ASKS ANDERSON, REFERRING TO HIS YOUNGER BROTHER.

"YOU KNOW YOUR BABY BROTHER".

"IS HE STILL GETTING HIGH AND LOOKING OUT THE WINDOW AT HIGH SCHOOL GIRLS WALKING THE SIDEWALK"?

"YES, TODAY IS FRIDAY. I'M SURE HE'S GOING TO REPEAT HIS DAILY ROUTINE".

"EXCUSE ME DR.GOLDMAN", SAYS NANCY.

"NANCY, CAN'T YOU SEE I'M ON THE PHONE"?

"WE HAVE A PATIENT NEEDING YOUR AS-SISTANCE. SHE DOESN'T HAVE AN APPOINT-MENT BUT SHE REALLY NEEDS TO SEE YOU TODAY. SHE SAID THAT SHE DOESN'T HAVE MUCH TIME—SHE HAS TO GET HER DAUGH-TER READY FOR THE DANCE AT SUMTER HIGH LATER TONIGHT. I KNOW THAT YOU SAID NOT TO SCHEDULE ANY MORE PATIENTS".

"THERE'S A DANCE LATER TONIGHT", ASKS DR. GOLDMAN SMILING. "HOW MANY PATIENTS DO I HAVE WAITING ON ME"?

"SEVEN"

"MAKE AN APPOINTMENT FOR HER TO SEE ME NEXT WEEK. I DON'T HAVE TIME FOR HER TODAY".

NANCY WALKS OUT AND TURNS AROUND. "I FORGOT TO MENTION…SHE'S BLACK, BUT SHE HAS INSURANCE".

DR. GOLDMAN SIGHS, TELL HER THAT I WILL FIT HER IN AFTER MY NEXT PATIENT".

"SON, DO YOU HAVE THAT PRIVATE JET FUELED AND READY TO TAKEOFF AT A MOMENT'S NOTICE"?

"NOT TONIGHT. IT'S OUR CHAIRMAN'S ANNIVERSARY. HE AND HIS WIFE WENT TO FLORIDA FOR THE WEEKEND".

"GET HERE SON. JUST GET HERE. I HAVE A FEELING TONIGHT YOUR BABY BROTHER WILL HAVE COMPANY, AND WE'LL HAVE EXACTLY WHAT WE NEED"!

DR. GOLDMAN CALLS RUDY MCDONALD, THE COUNTY CORONER.

"RUDY SPEAKING"!

"I NEED TO BORROW YOUR VAN".

"IT WILL BE PARKED IN MY YARD WITH THE KEYS UNDER THE FLOOR MAT".

CHAPTER 8

"I'LL GIVE YOU TWENTY DOLLARS IF YOU CAN PICK ME UP A 12 PACK OF BEER AND TWO BOT-TLES OF WINES", SAYS SHELTON.

"SHELTON, WHY ARE YOU OUT HERE TRYING TO BUY BEER? YOU SHOULD BE IN SCHOOL", ASKS JAMES.

STUTTERING, SHELTON LOOKS AT HIS SCHED-ULE. "I DIDN'T HAVE CLASS TODAY. MY SECOND JOB WAS NICE ENOUGH TO GIVE ME A DAY OFF".

"WHAT ARE YOU UP TO SHELTON? LET ME SEE WHAT YOU ARE READING"? JAMES GRABS THE SCHEDULE. "SHELTON, ACCORDING TO THIS SCHEDULE, YOU DID HAVE CLASS TODAY".

"I DID"?

"YES YOU DID".

"I'M GOING TO THE HIGH SCHOOL DANCE TO-NIGHT. I'LL BE 21 IN 7 MONTHS. I WANT TO CELEBRATE EARLY BY DRINKING A 12 PACK".

"YOU WANT TO CELEBRATE? SHELTON, YOU KNOW THIS GAS STATION IS THE AFTER HOURS HANGOUT SPOT. IT'S AN OUTDOOR CLUB FOR HIGH SCHOOL STUDENTS".

"WHEN I LEAVE THE DANCE TONIGHT, I PROM-ISE I WON'T COME THIS WAY".

"YOU PROMISE? ALRIGHT SHELTON, SINCE YOU'RE CELEBRATING, I'M GOING TO DO IT FOR YOU THIS TIME. BUT DON'T ASK ME AGAIN! WHERE'S MY TWENTY"?

CHAPTER 9

PATRICIA IS AT THE HIGH SCHOOL DANCE SPEAKING WITH MRS. LITTLE.

"PATRICIA, I KNOW AT TIMES CLASS CAN BE A LITTLE BORING TO YOU".

"THANK YOU MRS. LITTLE. I LOVE TO STUDY".

"WELL IT SHOWS".

"DID I TELL YOU I GOT ACCEPTED TO RICH-MOND COLLEGE IN TUSCALOOSA"?

"NO YOU DIDN'T. CONGRATULATIONS"!

"YEAH! I'M GOING TO BE A COMPUTER EXPERT SOMEDAY".

"PATRICIA, YOU CAN BE ANYTHING YOU WANT TO BE. YOU HAVE THE INTELLIGENCE".

CHAPTER 10

SHELTON IS AT THE DANCE, BUT IS IN THE BATHROOM PASSED OUT WITH A BEER IN HIS HAND. CHUCK BROWN, ANOTHER SENIOR ATTENDING SUMTER HIGH COMES INTO THE BATHROOM AND SEES SHELTON PASSED OUT.

"SHELTON, GET UP"!

"I DIDN'T DO IT! I DIDN'T DO IT", SCREAMS SHELTON.

"YOU'RE DRUNK SHELTON, SAYS CHUCK.

"YOU DON'T KNOW WHAT YOU'RE TALKING ABOUT! I'M NOT DRUNK, SAYS SHELTON AS HE FALLS BACK TO THE FLOOR.

"WHAT'S GOING ON"?, BILL WILLIAMS WALKS INTO THE BATHROOM AND ASKS.

"SHELTON IS DRUNK", SAYS CHUCK.

"I WOULDN'T WORRY ABOUT HIM", SAYS JIM. "HAVE YOU SEEN THE GIRLS IN THE DANCE"?

SHELTON GETS UP OFF THE FLOOR AND ASKS, "YOU THINK I CAN GET IN FREE"?

"YOU NEED TO TAKE YOUR BUTT HOME AND SLEEP IT OFF"!

"THERE'S A LONG LINE OF STUDENTS WAITING OUTSIDE TRYING TO GET IN THE DANCE".

CHAPTER 11

THE DANCE IS UNDERWAY, AND THE MUSIC IS LOUD. THE STUDENTS ARE DANCING AND HAVING FUN. SHELTON IS IN THE GYM AT THE DANCE, BUT HE HAS FALLEN TO THE FLOOR AGAIN. EVERYONE NOTICES THAT HE IS DRUNK AND IS LAUGHING.

"WHAT IS EVERYONE LAUGHING ABOUT", ASKS PATRICIA.

"SHELTON, IT SEEMS LIKE OUR HIGH SCHOOL JANITOR HAD TOO MUCH TO DRINK", SAYS CARLOS, ANOTHER SUMTER HIGH SCHOOL STUDENT.

"WELL, JUST DON'T STAND THERE! HELP HIM UP", SAYS PATRICIA.

"SHELTON, I THINK IT'S TIME FOR YOU TO HEAD HOME", SAYS CARLOS.

"SHELTON, CAN YOU WALK HOME", ASKS PATRICIA.

"I'M ONLY A COUPLE OF BLOCKS AWAY".

"CARLOS, TAKE SHELTON HOME".

"I'M NOT TAKING HIM HOME! I'M GOING TO DANCE"! CARLOS WALKS AWAY AND STARTS TO DANCE.

"SHELTON, YOU HAD TOO MUCH TO DRINK. DO YOU NEED A RIDE HOME"?

"I'M NOT READY TO GO HOME YET. I'M WAITING ON THE LAST PERSON TO LEAVE SO I CAN HAVE THE GYM CLEANED FOR P.E. CLASS ON MONDAY".

"SHELTON, YOU HAVE A KEY TO THIS GYMNASIUM. WHY DON'T YOU WAIT UNTIL TOMORROW"?

"I'LL BE FINE".

"IF YOU SAY SO". PATRICIA SEES CARLOS DANCING WITH ANOTHER GIRL, AND SAYS, "EXCUSE ME".

"NOT NOW, I LIKE THIS SONG, SAYS CARLOS.

PATRICIA WALKS AWAY UPSET.

"I'M SORRY PATRICIA", SAYS CARLOS.

"THIS IS OUR LAST HIGH SCHOOL DANCE FOR THE YEAR AND WHAT DO YOU DO? YOU DANCE WITH ANOTHER CHICK".

"BABY, IT'S NOT WHAT YOU THINK".

"OH REALLY, HOW IS IT THEN"?

"RENEE IS A CLASSMATE OF MINE. THAT'S IT".

"I CAN'T TELL CARLOS".

"SO NOW YOU'RE ACCUSING ME OF SEEING HER"?

"MAYBE RENEE IS THE REASON WHY WE HAVEN'T DANCED ALL NIGHT! JUST MAYBE RENEE IS THE REASON WHY YOU'RE NOT MAN ENOUGH TO TAKE SHELTON HOME"!

"LOOK, I DON'T HAVE TIME TO TAKE A MENTALLY RETARDED JANITOR HOME! YOU ARE TAKING THIS TOO FAR! RENEE AND I HAVE NOTHING IN COMMON"!

"REALLY, THEN EXPLAIN TO ME WHY SHE LEFT THIS LOVE LETTER ON YOUR CAR"?

"LOVE LETTER"?

"YES, LOVE LETTER CARLOS! YOU HAD ME FOOLED! YOU'VE NEVER LOVED ME! YOU'RE TOO BUSY LOVING YOURSELF"!

"PATRICIA WAIT", SCREAMS CARLOS.

THE DANCE NEARS AN END. CARLOS WALKS THROUGH THE CROWD LOOKING FOR PATRICIA. SHELTON STARTS TO CLEAN THE GYM AS THE CROWD BEGINS TO LEAVE. HE SEES PATRICIA IN A CORNER CRYING.

"PATRICIA, ARE YOU OKAY"?

"NO, I CAUGHT CARLOS CHEATING ON ME", CRIES PATRICIA.

"THAT DIRTY DOG", STUTTERS SHELTON

"SHELTON, WHY DO BOYS CHEAT"?

"ALL BOYS DON'T CHEAT, ONLY THE ONE'S WHO CAN'T GET ENOUGH", ANSWERS SHELTON.

"WE LOOKED SO GOOD TOGETHER. I THOUGHT HE WAS GOING TO BE MY HIGH SCHOOL SWEETHEART. I SAW OUR FUTURE TOGETHER. NOW IT'S OVER".

"YOU'LL BE JUST FINE. YOU'RE TOO SMART TO LET A BREAKUP RUIN YOUR LIFE".

"SHELTON, IT'S NOT THAT EASY FOR GIRLS. WE CAN'T GET OVER TRUE LOVE IN AN HOUR".

"I UNDERSTAND".

"I'M GOING OUTSIDE, ARE YOU OKAY SHELTON"?

"I'M FINE PATRICIA. I'M ABOUT TO LOCK UP THE GYM. CAN I WALK YOU TO THE GAS STATION"?

"I'LL BE FINE, SHELTON. ONE OF CARLOS' CLOSEST FRIENDS SAID CARLOS WAS COMING BACK TONIGHT TO EXPLAIN TO ME WHY RENEE LEFT A LOVE LETTER IN HIS CAR".

"HE WANTS TO COME BACK TONIGHT TO EXPLAIN TO YOU WHY HE CHEATED"?

"YES".

"OKAY, I'M GOING HOME".

SHELTON CLEANS THE GYM AND LEAVES FOR THE NIGHT. AS SHELTON HOLLOWAY WALKS DOWN THE SIDEWALK, TWO HIGH SCHOOL STUDENTS PUSH HIM TO THE GROUND.

"GET UP SHELTON", SAYS MICHAEL.

"I'M FINE, MICHEAL, I'M FINE. I'M GOING HOME".

"SHELTON, YOU'RE GOING THE WRONG WAY. YOU LIVE IN GRAND CITY RIGHT"?

"YEAH".

"GRAND CITY IS THAT DIRECTION", POINTS MICHEAL.

"OH YEAH, THANKS MICHEAL".

PATRICIA LOOKS AT HER WATCH AND SHAKES HER HEAD. "HE'S NOT COMING. MAYBE I SHOULD WAIT A LITTLE LONGER".

PATRICIA HANNAH WALKS DOWN THE SIDE-WALK. A VAN PULLS UP. TWO MEN JUMP OUT THE VAN AND ONE OF THEM HIT HER IN THE FACE WITH A SHOVEL.

CHAPTER 12

PATRICIA AWAKES TO FIND HERSELF TIED TO A CHAIR WITH A SHEET TIED AROUND HER HEAD. SHE BEGINS TO SCREAM.

"SOMEBODY HELP ME, HELP ME. PLEASE LET ME GO! PLEASE! WHAT DO YOU WANT FROM ME"?

DAVID GOLDMAN TAKES THE SHEET OFF HER HEAD AND WATCHES THE BLOOD RUN DOWN HER FACE.

PATRICIA REALIZES THAT SHE IS WEARING A DIFFERENT OUTFIT, AND SHE BEGINS TO SCREAM LOUDER. "WHERE ARE MY CLOTHES"?

DAVID GOLDMAN HOLDS THE BLUE JEANS AND T-SHIRT UP THAT PATRICIA WAS WEARING.

"GIVE ME MY CLOTHES"!

DAVID LIFTS THE CLOTHES TO HIS NOSE AND SMELLS THEM.

"SOMEONE HELP ME PLEASE"!

DAVID LOOKS AT PATRICIA'S DRIVERS LICENSE. "NO ONE CAN HEAR YOU". HE GRABS HER BY HER HAIR AND SAYS "LOOK, IT'S 3 AM. THERE'S NO ONE OUTSIDE".

"PLEASE DON'T HURT ME, PLEASE"!

"I'M NOT GOING TO HURT YOU PATRICIA. I PROMISE. YOU HAD THIS NUMBER IN YOUR POCKET. WHOSE NUMBER IS THIS"?

PATRICIA CRIES LOUDER. "MY MOM"!

DAVID PULLS OUT A TAPE RECORDER.

"WHAT ARE YOU DOING", ASKS PATRICIA.

"I WANT YOU TO BREATHE THROUGH THIS RE-CORDER. NO CONVERSATION. JUST BREATHE".

"FOR WHAT"? "YOU ARE SICK, YOU KNOW THAT"!

"PATRICIA, IF YOU WANT TO SEE YOUR MOTH-ER AGAIN, YOU'LL DO WHAT I SAY"!

PATRICIA BREATHES THROUGH THE TAPE RECORDER.

"GOOD GIRL. DO IT AGAIN".

PATRICIA BREATHES THROUGH THE TAPE RE-CORDER AGAIN.

ISABELLA, DAVID'S MOM, HEARS THE NOISE UP-STAIRS, AND ASKS HER HUSBAND WHAT WAS GOING ON.

"DAVID HAS A DATE TONIGHT WITH SOME BLACK GIRL. THAT'S ALL HONEY", SAYS DR. GOLDMAN.

DR. ANDERSON GOLDMAN ARRIVES AT THE HOME PANICKING BECAUSE HIS WIFE'S CON-DITION HAS WORSENED.

"SON, YOU'RE HERE", SAYS DR. GOLDMAN.

"DAD, I DIDN'T HAVE A CHOICE. MY WIFE HAS LESS THEN 36 HOURS TO LIVE".

"YOU GET THAT BLACK GIRL OUT OF MY HOUSE. YOU HEAR ME! GET HER OUT OF HERE", SCREAMS ISABELLA.

"WHERE IS SHE", DR. ANDERSON ASKS.

"SHE'S WITH YOUR BROTHER".

"WHY IS SHE WITH DAVID"?

"YOUR BROTHER JUST WANTED TO HAVE A LIT-TLE FUN WITH HER"

CHAPTER 13

PATRICIA LIES DEAD IN THE HOSPITAL BED.

"NOW THAT HER HEART IS REMOVED, IT MUST BE TRANSPLANTED INTO THE RECIPIENT WITHIN FOUR HOURS OR THE HEART MUSCLE WILL BE DAMAGED AND IT WILL NOT PUMP EFFICIENTLY. CONTACT YOUR WIFE'S DOCTORS AND TELL THEM TO PREPARE FOR SURGERY. WE HAVE A HEART", SAYS DR. GOLDMAN.

CHAPTER 14

SHELTON IS AT HOME IN THE BATHROOM RUNNING WATER OVER HIS FACE. HE WALKS FROM THE BATHROOM TO THE KITCHEN.

JACKIE, SHELTON'S SISTER, IS ALREADY AT THE TABLE EATING BREAKFAST.

"WHAT ARE YOU DOING HERE? WHERE'S MOM", ASKS SHELTON.

"SHE'S WHERE YOU SHOULD BE, ASLEEP. WHERE HAVE YOU BEEN"?

"BIG SISTER, I'M COMING FROM A DANCE", SHELTON SAYS AS HE OPENS THE CABINET TO GET A CAN OF TUNA.

"A DANCE"?

"YOU HEARD ME. I DIDN'T STUTTER"!

CHAPTER 15

AT YORK HOSPITAL, DR. GOLDMAN HAS PLACED PATRICIA'S ORGANS IN A COOLER AND IS PREPARING TO TRANSPORT THEM TO A SEPARATE HOSPITAL FOR HIS DAUGHTER-IN-LAW.

"HOW ARE WE PLANNING ON GETTING THIS HEART PASS SECURITY, ASKS DR. ANDERSON GOLDMAN.

"JUST LEAVE IT UP TO ME".

"I'M GETTING TIRED OF COVERING UP FOR THAT LITTLE BASTARD! EVERY TIME HE HAS THE URGE, WE HAVE TO END UP PAYING OFF PEOPLE AND YOU HAVE TO LEAVE TOWN. I THOUGHT WE SAID WE WEREN'T DOING THIS ANY MORE"?

"WE WOULDN'T BE IF YOUR WIFE DIDN'T NEED A HEART, REMEMBER. WE WOULD JUST BE GETTING RID OF A BODY. BESIDES, WE MADE A LOT OF MONEY SELLING THE ORGANS OF ALL

THOSE GIRLS HE JUST HAD TO HAVE. IT SET BOTH OF US UP FOR LIFE".

"WHY DON'T YOU JUST DO WHAT I SUGGESTED AND HAVE HIM PUT IN AN INSTITUTION. MY BROTHER IS SICK! I CAN'T EVEN TRUST HIM TO BE AROUND MY WIFE! HE'S THE REASON THAT I DON'T WANT TO HAVE KIDS".

"YOU KNOW QUITE WELL THAT WE CAN'T DO THAT. HE COULD GET TO TALKING. WE HAVE TO KEEP HIM WHERE WE CAN CONTROL WHO HE'S AROUND".

"WELL WE'RE NOT DOING A VERY GOOD JOB AT THAT, ARE WE"?

DAVID WALKS INTO THE ROOM SMELLING PATRICIA'S BLUE JEANS.

"SON, TAKE CARE OF THE BODY FOR ME", DR. GOLDMAN SAYS WHILE HE AND DR. ANDERSON WALK OUT WITH THE COOLER. "OH, I ALMOST FORGOT, HE THROWS THE KEYS, PARK THIS VAN IN THE DRIVEWAY ON 1987 HIGHTOWER AVENUE. PLEASE, LEAVE THE KEYS UNDER THE FLOOR MAT".

CHAPTER 16

HELEN IS PACING THE FLOOR AT HER HOME. SHE LOOKS AT HER WATCH, AND CALLS THE POLICE.

"911, HOW CAN I HELP YOU"?

"I'D LIKE TO REPORT MY DAUGHTER MISSING".

"HOW LONG HAS SHE BEEN MISSING"?

"SHE DIDN'T COME HOME FROM THE DANCE AT SUMTER HIGH SCHOOL LAST NIGHT".

"I'M SORRY MA'AM. ALABAMA LAW REQUIRES THAT A PERSON BE MISSING 24 HOURS BEFORE YOU CAN FILE A REPORT".

"24 HOURS"? "THAT'S TOO LONG"!

"WHERE WAS SHE LAST SEEN"?

"I TOLD YOU, SUMTER COUNTY HIGH! SHE ATTENDED THE DANCE LAST NIGHT".

"HAVE YOU TRIED CALLING ANY OF HER FRIENDS"?

"LISTEN, I KNOW MY DAUGHTER. SHE DOESN'T HAVE ANY FRIENDS".

"MA'AM, ARE YOU SURE YOUR DAUGHTER DIDN'T HAVE TOO MUCH TO DRINK"? MAYBE SHE SPENT THE NIGHT WITH A MALE COMPANION".

"SHE WOULD NEVER DO ANYTHING LIKE THAT. LET ME SPEAK TO AN OFFICER", SHOUTS HELEN.

"SURE, HOLD ON MA'AM".

"THIS IS SHERIFF PRICE SPEAKING".

"HELLO SHERIFF. MY DAUGHTER IS MISSING, AND YOUR OPERATOR IS TELLING ME THAT I CAN'T FILE A REPORT UNTIL SHE'S BEEN MISSING FOR 24 HOURS".

"OK, CALM DOWN! FIRST, WHAT'S YOUR DAUGHTER'S NAME"?

"PATRICIA ANN HANNAH".

"CAN YOU PLEASE DESCRIBE HER TO ME", ASKS SHERIFF PRICE.

"SHE'S 5FT 4IN AND 135 POUNDS, WITH LONG BLACK HAIR".

"OKAY, IS SHE BLACK OR WHITE"?

"SHE'S BLACK".

"DON'T WORRY MA'AM. WE'LL FILE A REPORT AND START LOOKING FOR HER. I'M GOING TO HAND YOU BACK OVER TO THE OPERATOR SO THAT SHE CAN GET SOME MORE INFORMATION FROM YOU".

CHAPTER 17

DR. GOLDMAN AND DR. ANDERSON GOLD-MAN ARE GOING THROUGH SECURITY AT THE AIRPORT.

DR. GOLDMAN SAYS, "SON, THIS FLIGHT SHOULD ONLY TAKE 30 MINUTES".

"I TALKED TO MY WIFE. "SHE SHOULD BE AT THE HOSPITAL BY NOW".

"GOOD, REMEMBER, IF ANYONE ASKS ABOUT IT, JUST SHOW THEM THE LETTER. YOU GOT THE COOLER"?

"YEAH, IT'S RIGHT HERE".

DR. ANDERSON GOLDMAN RUNS HIS LUGGAGE THROUGH SECURTIY.

CUSTOM SECURITY BRYANT, ASKS, "WHAT'S IN THE COOLER"?

"A LIVE ORGAN FOR TRANSPLANT. WE'RE BOTH DOCTORS AND THE RECIPIENT IS WAITING FOR THIS AT THE HOSPITAL", ANSWERS DR. GOLDMAN.

"SO YOU ARE..."?

"DR. ANDERSON GOLDMAN! HERE'S OUR DOCUMENTATION FOR THE ORGAN".

CUSTOM SECURITY BRYANT LOOKS AT LETTER SUSPICIOUSLY.

DR. GOLDMAN SAYS, "MR. BRYANT, I HAVE A PATIENT THAT I SAW THE OTHER DAY WHO TOLD ME THAT HER HUSBAND WORKS HERE AT THE AIRPORT DOING SECURITY. DO YOU KNOW SHIRLEY BRYANT"?

"THAT'S MY WIFE! SMALL WORLD! SHE TOLD ME THAT SHE DIDN'T HAVE AN APPOINTMENT AND THAT YOU STAYED LATE JUST TO SEE HER. THANK YOU, SIR! SHE'S DOING SO MUCH BETTER, BECAUSE OF YOU! HERE'S YOUR LETTER, SIR. HAVE A SAFE TRIP"!

CHAPTER 18

D.J. DADDY D IS ON THE SUMTER COUNTY RA-
DIO SHOW.

"IT'S A BEAUTIFUL SATURDAY MORNING,
CLEAR BLUE SKIES, HIGHS AROUND 80 DE-
GREES. BUT WE HAVE SAD NEWS TO REPORT
THIS MORNING. PATRICIA HANNAH, A STU-
DENT AT SUMTER COUNTY HIGH IS REPORTED
MISSING. SHE WAS LAST SEEN LAST NIGHT AT
THE SUMTER COUNTY HIGH SCHOOL DANCE
WEARING BLUE JEANS AND A WHITE BLOUSE.
IF YOU OR SOMEONE YOU KNOW HAVE ANY IN-
FORMATION ON HER DISAPPEARANCE, PLEASE
CALL SHERIFF PRICE'S OFFICE AT 334-392-1010".

CHAPTER 19

"I'M SORRY, MRS HANNAH, SAYS SHERIFF PRICE.".

"THIS IS NOT LIKE PATRICIA".

"HAS SHE HAD ANY DISAGREEMENTS WITH A FEMALE FRIEND OR BOYFRIEND"?

"NOT THAT I CAN THINK OF. THE ONLY FRIEND SHE HAS IS THE BOY SHE WAS DATING, CARLOS".

"CARLOS? WHAT IS HIS LAST NAME"?

"DUNLAP. CARLOS DUNLAP".

"I WILL BEGIN CONDUCTING INTERVIEWS OF STUDENTS THROUGHOUT SUMTER COUNTY HIGH".

"THANK YOU SHERIFF".

"IF YOU CAN THINK OF SOMETHING THAT COULD BE HELPFUL TO THE DISAPPERANCE OF YOUR DAUGHTER, PLEASE CALL ME". HE GIVES HER HIS BUSINESS CARD.

"I WILL SHERIFF".

"DON'T YOU WORRY MRS. HANNAH, WE'RE GOING TO FIND YOUR DAUGHTER".

SHERIFF PRICE LEAVES A MESSAGE ON DR. GOLDMAN'S PHONE. "I KNOW YOUR'RE PROBABLY OUT SOMEWHERE WITH YOUR WIFE ENJOYING THIS BEAUTIFUL DAY, BUT WE HAD A HOMICIDE TODAY. I HAD TO ADMIT, I WAS A LITTLE NERVOUS BECAUSE I THOUGHT IT WAS YOU, BUT IT SEEMS THAT WE MAY HAVE A FEW SUSPECTS LINED UP ALREADY—ALL BLACK. GUESS YOU WORKED YOUR LITTLE PROBLEM OUT ON YOUR OWN. ANYWAY, TELL THE WIFE I SAID HELLO".

CHAPTER 20

SHERIFF PRICE AND THE DEPUTY INTERVIEW SHELTON HOLLOWAY.

"DID YOU GO TO THE GREEK SHOW", ASKS SHERIFF PRICE.

"NO", REPLIES SHELTON.

"DID YOU STAY FOR THE ENTIRE GREEK SHOW"?

"YES".

"DID YOU GO TO THE DANCE"?

"YES".

"HOW DID YOU LEAVE THE DANCE"?

"WALKING".

THE DEPUTY ASKS, "WHO DID YOU SEE OUTSIDE THE GYM AFTER THE DANCE"?

BILL ANSWERS, "PATRICIA HANNAH"?

"WHO DID YOU SEE WITH HER", INQUIRES THE DEPUTY.

"SHELTON HOLLOWAY FOR A MINUTE, BUT THEN HE TOOK OFF WALKING. PEOPLE ARE SAYING THAT TWO STUDENTS, JANET THOMAS AND ANDREA MARTIN, SAW WHO TOOK PATRICIA".

"WHAT DO YOU MEAN"?

"THEY SAID THAT A VAN PULLED UP TO PATRICIA AND TWO MEN JUMPED OUT AND TOOK PATRICIA".

WELL WHY DON'T THEY COME FORWARD WITH THEIR STORY"?

"WORD IS THAT THEY HAVE BEEN THREATENED BY THE MEN IF THEY SAY ANYTHING TO THE POLICE".

SHERIFF PRICE BEGINS TO GET NERVOUS. "IT'S PROBABLY JUST A RUMOR. YOU'LL GET A LOT OF THAT. I'LL LOOK INTO IT FOR YOU. WHAT ARE THE WITNESSES NAMES"?

CHAPTER 21

ONE WEEK LATER, YORK POLICE DEPARTMENT BUILDING

"911, WHAT'S YOUR EMERGENCY"?

"I WORK AT ALABAMA POWER AND THERE'S A FOUL ODOR COMING BEHIND THE BUILDING".

POLICE OFFICERS ARRIVE AT THE MURDER SCENE. THE CORONER, RUDY MCDONALD, PULLS UP IN THE VAN.

"HELLO SHERIFF, WHAT DO WE HAVE HERE", ASKS RUDY.

"WE'VE BEEN EXPECTING YOU RUDY. SOME-ONE FROM THE ALABAMA POWER COMPANY CALLED IN A FOUL ODOR COMING FROM BE-HIND THEIR BUILDING".

"THIS BODY IS BADLY DECOMPOSED. I'LL HAVE TO IDENTIFY THIS VICTIM THROUGH DENTAL

RECORDS. ANY MISSING PERSONS OUT THERE THAT MATCH THE DESCRIPTION"

"I'M AFRAID IT MAY BE THE MISSING HIGH SCHOOL STUDENT WHO VANISHED ONE WEEK AGO. SHE'S THE ONLY MISSING PERSON THAT WE HAVE AT THIS TIME, SO WE CAN ASSUME IT'S HER. HER NAME IS PATRICIA ANN HAN-NAH. WE FOUND HER DIARY, DRIVER'S LICENSE AND SOME OTHER EVIDENCE. HER BLOUSE AND BRA ARE THERE AROUND HER NECK. HER BLUE JEANS AND TEE SHIRT WERE FOUND CLOSE TO HER BODY.

"WELL I'VE GOT MY WORK CUT OUT FOR ME. LET ME GET TO WORK.

"LET ME KNOW WHAT YOU FIND", REPLIES SHER-IFF PRICE. "I'VE GOT TO CATCH A MURDERER"!

CHAPTER 22

"THAT'S A SHAME, WHAT THEY DID TO PATRI-CIA. SHELTON DID YOU KNOW HER", INQUIRES SHELTON'S MOTHER.

"MOM, I SAW HER THE NIGHT OF THE DANCE".

"YOU DID"?

"SHE GOT INTO A FIGHT WITH CARLOS".

"CARLOS"? "WHO'S CARLOS", ASKS MRS. HOLLOWAY.

"HER BOYFRIEND".

THERE'S A HARD KNOCK ON THE DOOR. MRS. HOLLOWAY YELLS "COME IN".

"ARE YOU MRS. HOLLOWAY"?

"YES I AM. WHAT CAN I HELP YOU WITH"?

"I'M DAVID SCOTT WITH THE WELFARE DEPART-MENT. I WOULD LIKE TO SPEAK TO YOU ABOUT THE FOOD STAMPS YOU'RE RECEIVING".

"SHELTON, EXCUSE US FOR A MINUTE. THIS IS PERSONAL".

DAVID SHOWS PHOTOS OF CHARLES SIMPSON. "YOUR EX-HUSBAND, WAS RELEASED FROM PRISON 6 MONTHS AGO. IT SEEMS HE'S CUR-RENTLY WORKING A FULL TIME JOB FOR A CHICKEN FARM IN DECATUR, ALABAMA".

"WHAT DOES THAT HAVE TO DO WITH MY FOOD STAMPS"?

"ACCORDING TO OUR INVESTIGATION, YOU HAVE FIVE CHILDREN BY THREE DIFFERENT MEN".

"THAT'S CORRECT".

"WHERE'S TAMEKA, YOUR SIX YEAR OLD"?

"SHE'S WITH HER GRANDMOTHER".

"I'M AFRAID WE'RE GOING TO HAVE TO CUT OFF YOUR FOOD STAMPS. WE HAVE TOO MANY CONFLICTING STORIES".

"STOP ME FOR GETTING MY FOOD STAMPS? OH NO SIR! YOU NEED TO COME AGAIN! WHO DO YOU THINK YOU ARE? YOU CAN'T CUT OFF MY FOOD STAMPS! HOW AM I GONNA FEED MY FAMILY"?

"I'M SORRY MRS. HOLLOWAY. ACCORDING TO OUR RECORDS, YOU ARE ELIGIBLE TO MAKE CHARLES SIMPSON PAY YOU CHILD SUPPORT. YOU HAVE THIRTY DAYS TO FILE BEFORE YOUR FOOD STAMPS ARE CUT OFF".

"CHILD SUPPORT", WHAT IF HE QUITS HIS JOB"?

"I'M SORRY. HAVE A GOOD DAY".

MRS. HOLLOWAY FOLLOWS BEHIND HIM IN HER WHEELCHAIR. "WHO'S YOUR BOSS? I NEED TO SPEAK TO YOUR BOSS"!

"MOM, ARE YOU OKAY"?

"NO, I'M NOT OKAY. HE CUT OFF MY FOOD STAMPS"!

"HOW WE GOING TO EAT"?

"I DON'T KNOW SHELTON. I DON'T KNOW".

"DID I HEAR SOMETHING ABOUT CHILD SUPPORT"?

"YES. I CAN GO AFTER CHARLES TO MAKE HIM PAY ME CHILD SUPPORT".

"ARE YOU"?

"SHELTON, I DON'T KNOW HOW TO TELL YOU THIS. I DIDN'T HAVE TWO BABY DADDIES, I HAD THREE".

"WHAT"! SHELTON WALKS INTO THE KITCHEN SHAKING HIS HEAD IN DISBELIEF.

MRS. HOLLOWAY FOLLOWS HER SON IN HER WHEELCHAIR.

"WHY DID YOU LIE TO ME"?

"I DON'T KNOW. I THOUGHT IT WAS THE BEST THING TO DO AT THE TIME".

"DO MY SISTERS KNOW"?

"NO. I LIED TO THE STATE DEPARTMENT STATING THAT MY CHILDREN ONLY HAD TWO FATHERS".

"WHAT ARE WE GOING TO DO"?

"I DON'T KNOW SHELTON. ONE THING'S FOR SURE. I'M NOT ELIGIBLE FOR CHILD SUPPORT".

CHAPTER 23

"MRS. HANNAH THIS IS OUR CORONER, RUDY MC'DONALD. RUDY SHAKES HER HAND, BUT HE NEVER LOOKS MRS. HANNAH IN HER EYES.

"HELLO RUDY".

"THE DENTAL RECORDS THAT YOU POSITIVELY IDENTIFIED THE BADLY DECOMPOSED BODY AS YOUR 16 YEAR OLD DAUGHTER, PATRICIA ANN HANNAH. SHE HAD A TRAUMATIC HEAD IN-JURY. THE SKIN OF THE SCALP IS COMPLETELY AVULSED FROM THE SKULL WITH THE HAIR ATTACHED TO THE SKIN. HER EYES, LIPS AND TONGUE WERE COMPLETELY ABSENT AS WELL AS VARIOUS ORGANS".

TEARS DROP FROM MRS. HANNAH'S EYES.

"I'M SORRY", MRS. HANNAH, SAYS SHERIFF PRICE.

"SHE WAS ONLY 16 YEAR OLD! SHE HAD SUCH A BRIGHT FUTURE! MY ONLY CHILD! WHY WOULD SOMEONE DO THIS TO HER"?

"THAT'S WHAT I'M GOING TO FIND OUT. RUDY WANTS TO EXPLAIN TO YOU THE BRUISES HE FOUND ON HER NECK".

"MRS. HANNAH, I'M SO SORRY ABOUT YOUR LOSS. THERE'S NOTHING I CAN DO TO BRING HER BACK".

"THANK YOU RUDY. SHERIFF, WHERE DO WE GO FROM HERE"?

"WE HAVE A FEW LEADS. I'M GOING TO SUMTER COUNTY HIGH SCHOOL TODAY TO DO A SECOND INTERVIEW WITH THE STUDENTS WHO SAW HER AT THE DANCE".

"OKAY. WHAT HAPPENS IF NO ONE HAS SEEN ANYTHING"?

"SOMEONE IS GOING TO TALK. I'LL FIND PATRICIA'S KILLER"!

SHERIFF PRICE SITS IN HIS CAR AND TALKS ON HIS CELL PHONE TO DR. GOLDMAN.

"I CAN'T BELIEVE THAT YOU WENT AHEAD WITH IT! I KNEW IT WAS YOU AS SOON AS I

SAW THAT THE ORGANS WERE MISSING", SAYS
SHERIFF PRICE.

"DID SHE ASK WHY HER DAUGHTER'S ORGANS
WERE MISSING", ASK DR. GOLDMAN.

"NO. SHE'S TOO DEVASTATED TO THINK ABOUT
IT".

"GOOD. NOW THAT MY DAUGHTER IN LAW HAS
A NEW LEASE ON LIFE, I NEED YOU TO CLOSE
THIS CASE. FIND SOME POOR, NON-EDUCATED
BLACK MALE TO PLANT THIS MURDER ON".

"DONE, HAVE MY MONEY READY FOR ME IN A
SUITCASE. "I NEED MINE IN TWENTIES".

CHAPTER 24

SUMTER COUNTY RADIO STATION

"GOOD EVENING TO ALL MY PEOPLE OUT THERE. THIS IS D.J. DADDY D. WE REPORTED WEEKS AGO ABOUT THE DISAPPEARANCE AND MURDER OF SUMTER COUNTY HIGH SCHOOL STUDENT, PATRICIA HANNAH. THE YORK POLICE DEPARTMENT HAS A $20,000 REWARD TO ANYONE WHO HAS ANY INFORMATION LEADING TO THE CAPTURE AND CONVICTION OF HER MURDERER. IF YOU HEARD OR SEEN ANYTHING THAT NIGHT, PLEASE CALL THE YORK POLICE DEPARTMENT HEADQUARTERS. I CAN'T IMAGINE HOW SOMEONE COULD DO THIS TO THIS YOUNG, BEAUTIFUL GIRL".

CHAPTER 25

DAVID GOLDMAN CALLS MRS. HANNAH'S HOME. HE HOLDS THE TAPE RECORDER UP TO THE RECEIVER.

MRS. HANNAH IS LYING IN BED WHEN THE PHONE RINGS. SHE HEARS NOTHING BUT LOUD BREATHING IN THE PHONE. "PATRICIA, IS THAT YOU"? SHE BEGINS TO CRY. "COME HOME PLEASE! MOMMY LOVES YOU"! THE PHONE GOES DEAD.

THE NEXT MORNING AT MRS. HANNAH'S HOME, SHE TELLS THE SHERIFF ABOUT THE PHONE CALLS.

"SHERIFF, I KNOW IT WAS PATRICIA"!

"WHAT DID THE CALLER SAY"?

"IT WAS PATRICIA CRYING FOR HELP. I KNOW HER VOICE".

"MRS. HANNAH, IT WASN'T PATRICIA. PATRI-CIA IS DEAD".

"CAN YOU TRACE THE CALL"?

"IT WOULDN'T DO ANY GOOD. I'M ON MY WAY TO INTERVIEW STUDENTS AGAIN".

"ANY LUCK"?

"NOT YET, MOST OF THE STUDENTS DIDN'T SEE HER AFTER THE DANCE".

CHAPTER 26

YORK POLICE DEPARTMENT OFFICE

THE DEPUTY CONTINUES TO INTERVIEW STU-
DENTS WHO ATTENDED THE DANCE THAT
NIGHT.

"DID YOU SEE PATRICIA THAT NIGHT", IN-
QUIRES THE DEPUTY.

CHUCK BROWN, ANOTHER STUDENT, AN-
SWERS "YES! SHE HAD AN ARGUMENT WITH
CARLOS".

"WHO IS CARLOS"? WHAT HIS LAST NAME",
ASKS THE SHERIFF.

"DUNLAP! HE WAS HER BOYFRIEND! WE IN-
TERVIEWED HIM TWICE. THERE'S NOTHING
THERE. HE HAS A STRONG ALIBI.

"WHAT DID YOU DO WHEN YOU SAW THE COU-
PLE ARGUING", ASKS THE DEPUTY.

"I KEPT ON DANCING", REPLIED CHUCK.

THE SHERIFF WALKS TO THE WINDOW AND SEES SHELTON OUTSIDE SMILING. "WHY IS THIS GUY ALWAYS HANGING AROUND"?

SHERIFF PRICE YELLS TO SHELTON THROUGH THE WINDOW. "MR. HOLLOWAY, WE INTERVIEWED YOU SEVERAL TIMES AND YOU REFUSE TO GO HOME. IS THERE SOMETHING YOU'RE NOT TELLING US"?

"I SAW WHO KILLED PATRICIA HANNAH".

SHERIFF PRICE BRINGS SHELTON BACK INTO HIS OFFICE. "TAKE A SEAT MR. HOLLOWAY".

"YOU'RE WASTING YOUR TIME WITH THIS GUY. WE INTERVIEWED HIM SEVERAL TIMES. HE DOESN"T HAVE COMMON SENSE", SAYS THE DEPUTY.

"ISN'T HE THE MENTALLY CHALLENGED STUDENT I ALREADY INTERVIEWED"?

"YES, HE'S IN SPECIAL ED. HE'S ALSO A JANITOR AT SUMTER COUNTY HIGH SCHOOL".

"MAYBE HE'S READY TO TALK THIS TIME".

"OKAY, BUT I THINK THAT IT'S A DEAD END".

"MR. HOLLOWAY PLEASE TAKE ME BACK TO THE NIGHT OF THE HIGH SCHOOL DANCE. DID YOU SEE PATRICIA HANNAH", ASKS SHERIFF PRICE.

"WHAT YOU MEAN TAKE ME BACK. WHAT DOES THAT MEAN"?

"DID YOU SEE PATRICIA HANNAH"?

"I SAW HER WALKING DOWN THE HALL".

"SO YOU DID SEE HER"?

"I SEE HER AT SCHOOL EVERYDAY".

"I TOLD YOU, NO COMMON SENSE", SAYS THE DEPUTY.

SHERIFF PRICE WALKS AWAY TO GET A CUP OF COFFEE. HE LOOKS AROUND THE ROOM THINKING. "PERFECT".

THE SHERIFF'S OPERATOR INTERUPTS. "EXCUSE ME SHERIFF PRICE, DR. GOLDMAN IS ON LINE 3".

"SHERIFF PRICE SPEAKING".

"HAVE YOU FOUND OUR GUY", ASKS DR. GOLDMAN"

"NOT YET. IT'S NOT THAT EASY".

"WHAT DO YOU MEAN IT'S NOT THAT EASY? HOW HARD IS IT TO FIND A NON-EDUCATED BLACK MAN TO BLAME? WHAT AM I PAYING YOU FOR"?

"I THINK I JUST DID. LET ME CALL YOUR BACK".

"SHELTON, IS THERE A REASON WHY YOU LIKE HANGING AROUND? WHERE ARE YOUR PARENTS"?

"MY DADDY IS DEAD. MY MOMMA, SHE'S HOME TRYING TO FIGURE OUT A WAY TO GET BACK ON FOOD STAMPS".

"DO YOU HAVE ANY BROTHERS OR SISTERS"?

"FOUR SISTERS, I'M THE ONLY BOY".

"WHAT IF I COULD ASSIST YOUR FAMILY WITH FINANCIAL HELP"?

"FINANCIAL HELP? WHAT'S A FINANCIAL HELP"?

"THAT'S WHEN SOMEONE OFFERS YOU MONEY TO HELP WHATEVER SITUATION YOU'RE IN".

"MONEY, I LIKE MONEY! MY MOMMA NEEDS MONEY! HOW MUCH"?

THE SHERIFF PATS SHELTON ON HIS SHOULDER AND SHAKES HIS HEAD. NEVER MIND SHELTON, NEVER MIND. GO HOME. PLEASE GO HOME".

CHAPTER 27

PROSECUTOR, RICHARD STOKELY'S OFFICE

PROSECUTOR RICHARD STOKELY SPEAKS TO MRS. HOLLOWAY. "MRS. HOLLOWAY! I UNDERSTAND YOU CAN'T READ OR WRITE".

"YES", ANSWERS MRS. HOLLOWAY. "CAN'T NONE OF MY KIDS READ OR WRITE".

"DID YOU SEE YOUR SON THE NIGHT PATRICIA HANNAH WAS MURDERED"?

"NO, BUT MY DAUGHTER DID. SHE FOUND HIM SLEEPING ON HER PORCH THE MORNING AFTER PATRICIA DISAPPEARED. BUT THE DAY THAT PATRICIA'S BODY WAS FOUND, HE STAYED IN ALL NIGHT. HE NEVER STAYS IN ALL NIGHT. HE ALWAYS GOES OUT AT NIGHT".

"SO YOU'LL TELLING ME THE NIGHT PATRICIA HANNAH WAS FOUND, YOUR SON CAME HOME AND HE HASN'T LEFT SINCE"?

"YES", REPLIES MRS. HOLLOWAY.

CHAPTER 28

MRS. HANNAH IS AT HOME WHEN THE DOOR-BELL RINGS. PAMELA, A GOOD FRIEND AND NEIGHBOR IS AT THE DOOR.

"I'M SORRY. SHE DIDN'T DESERVE THIS", CRIES PAMELA.

"COME IN PAM".

"MY HUSBAND AND I SAW HER PICTURE ON THE NEWS LAST NIGHT. WE COULDN'T BE-LIEVE IT".

"YEAH, IT SEEMS LIKE A DREAM. I WOULD NEV-ER IMAGINE SOMEONE WOULD KILL MY ONLY DAUGHTER. I DON'T KNOW WHO TO TRUST"!

"DID THE CORONER SAY WHAT HAPPENED TO HER BODY"?

"HE WAS TALKING ABOUT THINGS THAT I DIDN'T UNDERSTAND. I DON'T TRUST HIM. HE

NEVER LOOKS ME IN MY EYES WHEN HE TALKS TO ME".

"MAYBE HE KNOWS SOMETHING".

"YOU MIGHT BE RIGHT".

CHAPTER 29

SHELTON RETURNS HOME AND ALL OF THE LIGHTS ARE OFF.

"WHERE HAVE YOU BEEN ALL DAY", ASKS SHELTON'S MOTHER.

"WHAT HAPPENED TO THE LIGHTS"?

"DID YOU HERE ME? I SAID WHERE HAVE YOU BEEN"?

"I WAS AT THE POLICE STATION".

"FOR WHAT"?

"THE SHERIFF WANTED TO KNOW DID I SEE PATRICIA HANNAH THE NIGHT AT THE DANCE".

"DID YOU"?

"YEAH, I SAW HER. SHE HELPED ME UP OFF THE FLOOR. ARE YOU GOING TO TELL ME WHAT HAPPEN TO OUR LIGHTS"?

"WHAT YOU THINK HAPPENED TO OUR LIGHTS, SHELTON? I DON'T HAVE ANY MONEY TO PAY THE BILL. HERE. GET USED TO THIS. MRS. HOLLOWAY PASS SHELTON A CANDLE. WHAT DID THE SHERIFF SAY"?

"I CAN'T LIVE LIKE THIS"! SHELTON SLAMS THE DOOR.

MRS. HOLLOWAY SHOUTS THROUGH THE DOOR, "WHAT CAN YOU DO? YOU DON'T HAVE MONEY, FOOD OR ANY PLANS TO GET US OUT THIS MESS! HELL, YOU CAN'T HELP ME! I'LL BE HELPING YOU FOR THE REST OF MY LIFE"!

CHAPTER 30

MRS. HANNAH IS LYING ON THE BED WHEN THE PHONE RINGS. A LOUD BREATHING IS HEARD. "PATRICIA, MOMMY LOVES YOU. COME HOME! PLEASE COME HOME! I MISS YOU".

THE NEXT MORNING

SHERIFF PRICE COMMENTS, "I THINK THE NIGHT SHE WAS ABDUCTED THE KILLER RECORDED THE INCIDENT".

MRS. HANNAH REPLIES, "I HOPE YOU GET THIS GUY".

SHERIFF PRICE PAGER RINGS. HE SEES A NUMBER COMING FROM HIS OFFICE AND ASK MRS. HANNAH COULD HE USED HER HOME PHONE.

"DR. GOLDMAN IS REQUESTING TO SEE YOU IMMEDIATELY. HE SAID IT'S VERY IMPORTANT", SAYS THE OPERATOR.

SHERIFF PRICE RETURNS TO THE YORK PO-
LICE STATION TO MEET WITH DR. GOLDMAN.
WHEN SHERIFF PRICE ARRIVES, DR. GOLDMAN
IS SITTING IN HIS CAR.

SHERIFF PRICE STANDS OUTSIDE OF DR. GOLD-
MAN'S CAR. "WHAT IS SO IMPORTANT THAT
YOU NEED TO TALK TO ME ABOUT? THIS IS AN
OPEN INVESTIGATION! LET ME DO MY JOB".

DR. GOLDMAN ROLLS DOWN THE WINDOW.
"SHUT UP AND GET IN THE CAR". HE REACHES
TO THE BACK SEAT AND PUTS A BRIEFCASE IN
SHERIFF PRICE'S LAP. "THERE'S FIFTY THOU-
SAND DOLLARS CASH IN THAT BRIEFCASE".

SHERIFF PRICE TRIES TO OPEN IT.

"DON'T OPEN IT"!

"GREEN IS MY FAVOR COLOR. I THOUGHT I
TOLD YOU TO MAKE SURE THE BRIEFCASE IS
GREEN".

"IT DOESN'T MATTER WHAT THE OUTSIDE
LOOKS LIKE. ALL THAT MATTERS IS WHAT
THE INSIDE LOOKS LIKE. THE INSIDE IS GREEN.
FIFTY THOUSAND DOLLARS GREEN! ALL
TWENTIES".

"THAT'S ENOUGH MONEY TO BUY ME A NEW HOME IN DEMOPOLIS".

"SHERIFF, WHEN YOU FIND OUR GUY, THAT'S THE DAY YOU'LL GET THIS CASH".

SHERIFF PRICE LOOKS SURPRISED. "WHAT THE"... HE SEES MRS. HOLLOWAY COMING DOWN THE SIDEWALK IN HER WHEELCHAIR.

MRS. HOLLOWAY IS ON THE SIDEWALK IN HER WHEELCHAIR HEADED TO THE POLICE STATION TO TURN HER SON IN TO COLLECT THE REWARD MONEY.

"I NEED TO SEE THE SHERIFF", DEMANDS MRS. HOLLOWAY.

"AND WHO ARE YOU", ASKS THE DEPUTY.

"I'M MRS. HOLLOWAY. SHELTON'S MOTHER, BUT EVERYONE KNOWS HIM AROUND HERE AS CHEESE. I KNOW WHO KILLED PATRICIA HANNAH".

THE DEPUTY WALKS OVER TO THE SHERIFF AND LOOKS BACK AT MRS. HOLLOWAY. "SHERIFF, YOU WON'T BELIEVE THIS! WE HAVE MRS. HOLLOWAY, THE MOTHER OF SHELTON HOLLOWAY, AKA CHEESE. SHE CLAIMS SHE KNOWS WHO KILLED PATRICIA HANNAH".

"MRS. HOLLOWAY, I'M SHERIFF PRICE OF YORK POLICE DEPARTMENT. I UNDERSTAND YOU HAVE INFORMATION ABOUT PATRICIA HANNAH'S MURDERER"?

"YES I DO. FIRST, I WOULD LIKE TO KNOW IF I GIVE YOU THIS INFORMATION, WILL MY FAMILY BE PROTECTED".

"THAT'S GUARANTEED", ANSWERS THE SHERIFF.

"SECONDLY, I HEARD ON THE RADIO THAT THERE WAS A REWARD".

"THAT'S CORRECT. THERE IS A $20,000 REWARD".

"AND YOU SURE MY FAMILY AND I WILL BE PROTECTED"?

"YOU HAVE MY WORD MRS. HOLLOWAY".

"MY SON".

"COME AGAIN"?

"MY SON, SHELTON JEROME HOLLOWAY KILLED PATRICIA HANNAH".

"HOW DO YOU KNOW THIS"?

"MY SON WAS AT THAT DANCE CLAIMING HE WAS WAITING ON ALL THE STUDENTS TO LEAVE SO HE COULD CLEAN UP THE GYM. HE WASN'T WAITING ON THOSE STUDENTS TO LEAVE".

"ARE YOU TELLING ME YOU'RE SON, SHELTON

JEROME HOLLOWAY, WAS WAITING ON PATRI-CIA TO LEAVE SO HE COULD KILL HER"?

"THAT'S EXACTLY WHAT I'M TELLING YOU"!

"MRS. HOLLOWAY, YOU JUST MADE YOURSELF $20,000"!

CHAPTER 31

SUMTER COUNTY RADIO STATION

"THIS IS DJ DADDY D". WE HAVE BREAKING NEWS FROM THE YORK POLICE DEPARTMENT. SHELTON JEROME HOLLOWAY, A MENTALLY RETARDED SUMTER COUNTY HIGH SCHOOL JANITOR, IS A MURDER SUSPECT IN THE DEATH OF PATRICIA HANNAH. SOUNDS LIKE THE PO-LICE ARE TRYING TO CLOSE THIS CASE! OUR PHONE LINES ARE BLOWING UP OVER THIS ONE! YOU'RE LIVE WITH DJ DADDY D CALLER! GO AHEAD WITH YOUR COMMENT".

CHAPTER 32

"SHERIFF, WE ARE GETTING A HIGH VOLUME OF CALLS ON THIS GUY", SAYS THE DEPUTY, AS HE POINTS TO SHELTON HOLLOWAY WHO IS SITTING DOWN WITH HANDCUFFS ON. "I WENT OVER TO ARREST SHELTON HOLLOWAY, AND READ HIM HIS MIRANDA RIGHTS. I DON'T THINK THAT HE UNDERSTOOD WHAT I WAS TALKING ABOUT".

"SO DID HE WAIVE HIS RIGHTS", ASKS THE SHERIFF.

"YES".

"WHAT ARE THE CALLERS SAYING"?

"THEY SAY THIS GUY DOESN'T HAVE COMMON SENSE. THAT HE WOULDN'T HURT A FLY".

"COMMON SENSE, HUH! TAKE HIM TO HIS JAIL CELL".

DR. GOLDMAN WALKS IN WITH THE BRIEFCASE IN HIS HAND.

"DEPUTY, WE'RE DONE FOR THE DAY. YOU CAN HEAD HOME NOW".

"THANK YOU SHERIFF". HE WALKS SHELTON JEROME HOLLOWAY OUT WHILE DR. GOLDMAN STANDS WITH THE BRIEFCASE.

"HOW DID YOU GET HIM", ASKS DR. GOLDMAN.

"IT WAS BETTER THAN I COULD'VE IMAGINED! HIS MOTHER GAVE HIM UP! SHE SAID HE KILLED PATRICIA HANNAH! IT WAS LIKE SHE HANDED HIM TO US ON A SILVER PLATTER"!

"HE LOOKS LIKE OUR GUY"!

"HAVE YOU LISTENED TO RADIO OR THE NEWS? HELL, THESE PEOPLE IN THIS CITY ARE UPSET WITH MY DEPARTMENT RIGHT NOW. THEY DON'T BELIEVE THAT HE COULD'VE DONE IT! I DON'T KNOW WHAT TO CHARGE SHELTON HOLLOWAY WITH, AND HE DOESN'T KNOW WHY HE'S SITTING IN JAIL".

"MURDER? " YOU CHARGED HIM WITH MUR-DER? LOOK, I DON'T GIVE A DAMN ABOUT WHAT THESE PEOPLE ARE SAYING! ARE YOU

THE LAW, OR ARE THE PEOPLE CALLING THE SHOTS AROUND HERE"?

"YEAH, BUT YOU'RE NOT THE ONE THE F.B.I. WOULD COME SNOOPING AROUND. HELL, I DON'T EVEN HAVE A CASE. ALL I HAVE IS A MOTHER IN A WHEELCHAIR SAYING HER SON IS GUILTY OF THIS CRIME".

"LIVING IN ALABAMA, ALL OF YOUR LIFE IS CATCHING UP WITH YOU SHERIFF. LOOK, ALL YOU HAVE TO DO IS TIE THE EVIDENCE TO HIM. AND CALL REV. WILLIE".

"WHY WOULD I CALL A BLACK PREACHER"?

"WE'LL PAY THEIR LEADER OFF. HE WILL KEEP THE BLACKS QUIET".

"THAT'S NOT GOING TO WORK. HE'S NEVER GOING TO GO FOR THAT"!

"SHUT UP, SHERIFF! HE'S DONE IT BEFORE! JUST LISTEN TO ME AND EVERYTHING WILL GO EX-ACTLY AS PLANNED"!

"TOMORROW, 9A.M. SHARP, YOU WILL HAVE SHELTON HOLLOWAY IN MONTGOMERY, ALABAMA SHOPPING WITH YOU AND YOUR DEPUTY".

"SHOPPING"?

"YES, SHOPPING, YOU'LL MAKE HIM THINK HE'S GETTING MONEY AND NEW CLOTHES FOR SAYING THAT HE KILLED PATRICIA HANNAH. HE'S NOT TOO SMART, RIGHT? DIDN'T YOU SAY HE HAS A LOW IQ"?

"I HEARD THAT HIS IQ IS PRETTY LOW".

"DON'T WORRY. I'LL GET AN EXPERT TO SAY THAT IT IS MUCH HIGHER, AND THAT HE KNEW EXACTLY WHAT HE WAS DOING. YOUR DEPUTY WILL FEED MR. HOLLOWAY TO MAKE HIM FEEL COMFORTABLE".

"YOU WILL QUESTION MR. HOLLOWAY FOR HOURS USING SEVERAL DIFFERENT TAPES. I'M SURE HE PROBABLY WILL SAY HE'S NOT GUILTY OF THIS CRIME AT FIRST, BUT IF YOU KEEP PRESSING HIM, HE'LL EVENTUALLY GIVE IN. ON ONE OF THOSE TAPES HE HAS TO ADMIT THAT HE KILLED PATRICIA HANNAH".

"WHAT IF WE NEVER GET HIM TO SAY HE DIDN'T KILL HER"?

"YOU THREATEN HIS FAMILY. TELL HIM YOU ARE GOING TO TAKE HIS FAMILY OUT OF TOWN TO KILL THEM IF HE DOESN'T CONFESS TO THIS CRIME".

"WHAT HAPPENS AFTER THAT"?

"THAT WILL BE YOUR CONFESSION TAPE. WITH OUR EXPERT TESTIMONY, WE WILL PROVE THAT SHELTON JEROME HOLLOWAY IS STREET SMART, NOT MENTALLY RETARDED, AND CAPABLE OF MURDER".

CHAPTER 33

THE NEXT MORNING IN MONTOGOMERY, ALA-
BAMA, SHELTON IS TRYING ON NEW CLOTHES.
"Y'ALL BEEN SO NICE TO ME, I'M GOING TO HELP
YOU SOLVE THIS CRIME. I SAW PATRICIA THAT
NIGHT OF THE SCHOOL DANCE".

"YOU LIKE YOU'RE OUTFIT SHELTON", ASKS
THE SHERIFF.

"YEAH, THIS IS NICE".

"LET'S HURRY UP. YOU HAVE AN APPOINTMENT
WAITING FOR YOU AT THE HOTEL".

AT THE MOTEL, THE SHERIFF PURCHASED
A CHEESEBURGER, FRIES AND SODA FOR
SHELTON.

"I DON'T LIKE THIS SHERIFF, SAYS THE
DEPUTY.

"YOU'LL BE JUST FINE. JUST THINK, I WILL RE-TIRE SOON AND THIS WILL BE ALL YOURS. DO YOU HAVE THE DRUGS"?

"RIGHT HERE", THE DEPUTY SAYS AND POURS THE DRUGS IN THE DRINK.

SHELTON IS ON THE BED EATING A CHEESE-BURGER AND DRINKING HIS SODA. "THIS IS GOOD, ANY KETCHUP IN THAT BAG"?

"HERE YOU GO, SHELTON. NOW I NEED TO ASK YOU SOME QUESTIONS ABOUT THE NIGHT THAT PATRICIA HANNAH WAS KILLED".

"OKAY, CAN I FINISH THIS BURGER? IT'S PRETTY GOOD". HE DRINKS THE SODA.

CHAPTER 34

"THAT WAS BRAVE OF YOU TO TURN YOUR SON IN". THE SHERIFF SAYS WHILE SPEAKING TO MRS. HALLOWAY.

"I HAD TO. MY CONSCIENCE WAS BOTHERING ME".

"I WILL BE BACK IN TOWN LATER TODAY. ONCE WE GET A CONFESSION FROM YOUR SON I WILL BE ABLE TO GIVE YOU YOUR REWARD MONEY".

"THANK YOU! THANK YOU, SHERIFF. THE CHECK IS ALL I NEED"!

"SHELTON, YOU REMEMBER THE NIGHT PATRICIA HANNAH WAS MURDERED", THE SHERIFF ASKS AS HE PULLS OUT THE VIDEO RECORDER.

"YES".

"WHAT DID YOU DO"?

"NOTHING, I REMEMBER I WAS WALKING HOME DRUNK AND I PASSED OUT ON THE SIDEWALK".

"NO SHELTON, YOU KILLED PATRICIA HANNAH"!

"I DIDN'T DO IT. I DIDN'T DO IT"!

"YES YOU DID, SHELTON. YOU SEXUALLY ABUSED HER, KILLED HER AND THREW HER BODY OUT LIKE TRASH BEHIND THE ALABAMA POWER BUILDING".

"I DIDN'T, I LOVE THAT GIRL", CRIES SHELTON.

"YES, YOU LOVE HER! YOU WANTED A RELA-TIONSHIP WITH HER, BUT SHE DIDN'T WANT YOU"!

SHELTON BEGINS TO STUTTER AND CRIES HARDRER. "THAT'S NOT TRUE! SHE WAS ONE OF THE ONLY STUDENT AT SUMTER COUNTY HIGH WHO CARED ABOUT ME! I WOULDN'T HURT HER LIKE THAT"!

"YOU'RE LYING TO ME SHELTON, AND YOU KNOW IT! NOW IF YOU DON'T DO WHAT I TELL YOU I WILL KILL YOU AND YOUR FAMILY"!

"I DON'T KNOW WHAT YOU'RE TALKING ABOUT".

THE DEPUTY HOLDS THE VIDEO RECORDER UP TO SHELTON'S MOUTH. "ADMIT IT SHELTON! YOU KILLED PATRICIA HANNAH"!

"I DIDN'T KILL HER".

"SAY IT, SHELTON! YOU KILLED PATRICIA HANNAH"!

"I DIDN'T KILL HER".

"THIS IS YOUR LAST WARNING, SHELTON! YOU AND YOUR FAMILY WILL BE KILLED"!

"PLEASE DON'T HURT MY MOM! SHE'S ALL I HAVE! JUST PLEASE DON'T HURT HER. OK, I DID IT"!

SURPRISED, THE DEPUTY ASKS, "WHAT? WHAT DID YOU SAY SHELTON"?

TEARS STREAMING DOWN HIS FACE, SHELTON SAYS, "I KILLED PATRICIA HANNAH". SHELTON'S HEAD DROPS INTO THE PILLOW.

THE DEPUTY AND THE SHERIFF WALK INTO ANOTHER ROOM.

"GOOD JOB. NOW WE'RE GOING TO MAKE IT LOOK LIKE SHELTON BROKE OUT OF JAIL. CALL MRS. HANNAH AND TELL HER SHELTON BROKE OUT OF JAIL AND THAT HE WAS LAST SEEN WALKING DOWNTOWN YORK WITH SOME OF PATRICIA'S THINGS IN A BROWN BAG".

"I'LL MAKE THE CALL, SAYS THE DEPUTY.

CHAPTER 35

SHELTON WALKS INTO THE COURTROOM IN HANDCUFFS WITH THE SHERIFF.

"WAIT A MINUTE; HE WANTS TO TAKE A PICTURE OF ME. I GOT TO LOOK MY BEST", SAYS SHELTON. "MAKE SURE YOU GET THIS SIDE. THIS IS MY GOOD SIDE".

MEDIA TONY DOUGLASS TAKES THE PICTURE. "THIS GUY DOESN'T HAVE A CLUE WHY HE'S HERE".

"ALL RISE, COURT IS NOW IN SESSION. THE HONORABLE JUDGE LEVY PRESIDING", ANNOUNCES THE BAILIFF.

JUDGE LEVY WALKS IN. "YOU MAY BE SEATED. STATE OF ALABAMA VS SHELTON JEROME HOLLOWAY AKA CHEESE ACCUSED OF CAPITAL MURDER TWO COUNTS OF A 16 YEAR OLD MINOR PATRICIA ANN HANNAH. MR. HOLLOWAY, HOW DO YOU PLEAD"?

MICHEAL RUSSO SAYS, "MY CLIENT PLEADS NOT GUILTY, YOUR HONOR".

"MR RUSSO, YOUR CLIENT SHELTON JEROME HOLLOWAY WAS FOUND GUILTY LAST APRIL OF ATTEMPTED BURGLARY IN THE THIRD DEGREE. HIS BAIL WILL BE REVOKED. YOU MAKE CALL YOUR FIRST WITNESS".

"YOUR HONOR, I WOULD LIKE TO CALL THE CORONER, MR. RUDY MC'DONALD TO THE WITNESS STAND", SAYS MICHEAL. "CAN YOU IDENTIFY FOR THE RECORD, YOUR NAME AND YOUR JOB TITLE"?

"MY NAME IS RUDY MC'DONALD. I AM THE CORONER FOR SUMTER COUNTY".

"MR. MC'DONALD, DESCRIBE THE JOB OF A CORONER".

"THE MAIN DUTY OF A CORONER OR A MEDICAL EXAMINER IS TO ENQUIRE INTO SUDDEN OR UNEXPLAINED DEATHS. USUALLY A POST MORTEM EXAMINATION IS PERFORMED, FOLLOWED BY AN INQUEST, IF THE CAUSE OF DEATH IS NOT NATURAL".

"FOLLOWED BY AN INQUEST IF THE CAUSE OF DEATH IS NOT NATURAL? WHEN YOU EXAM-

INED PATRICIA HANNAH'S BODY, WHAT WAS HER CAUSE OF DEATH"?

"PATRICIA HANNAH HAD A TRAUMATIC HEAD INJURY. EVIDENCE SUGGESTS THAT SHE WAS ABDUCTED BY FORCE, CAUSING HER TO FIGHT FOR HER LIFE. SHE WAS ALSO RAPED BEFORE SHE WAS KILLED. HER LIVER, KIDNEYS, HEART AND EYES WERE THEN REMOVED FROM HER BODY".

"DO YOU THINK A MENTALLY RETARDED MALE WITH AN IQ OF 40 COULD COMMITT SUCH A CRIME AS THIS"?

"OBJECTION YOUR HONOR, HE'S A MEDICAL EX-AMINER NOT A PSYCHOLOGIST", ARGUES PROS-ECUTOR RICHARD STOKELY.

"OVERRULED, PROCEED".

"DO YOU THINK SHELTON HOLLOWAY A MEN-TALLY RETARDED MALE WITH AN IQ OF 40 COULD SURGICALLY REMOVE A LIVER, KIDNEY, EYES AND A HEART"?

"NO, I DON'T THINK MR. HOLLOWAY WOULD BE ABLE TO COMMITT TO A CRIME LIKE THIS".

SHERIFF PRICE IS IN THE COURTROOM AND GIVES RUDY MCDONALD A SERIOUS LOOK.

"FROM YOUR EXPERIENCE AS MEDICAL EXAM-INERS, WHAT KIND OF PERSON DO YOU THINK KILLED PATRICIA HANNAH"?

"OBJECTION YOUR HONOR"!

"OVERRULED"!

"SOMEONE WHO WOULD HAVE EXPERIENCE IN THE REMOVAL OF ORGANS", SAYS RUDY.

"NO FURTHER QUESTIONS, YOUR HONOR".

"MR. STOKELY". THE JUDGE SAYS AFTER HE NO-TICES THE SHERIFF SPEAKING IN THE PROS-ECUTOR'S EAR.

"MR. STOKELY"!

"THE PROSECUTOR HAS NO QUESTIONS FOR THIS WITNESS AT THIS TIME".

"YOU MAY STEP DOWN MR. MC'DONALD. WE WILL TAKE A 30 MINUTE RECESS".

OUTSIDE OF THE COURTROOM, SHERIFF PRICE PUSHES MR.MC'DONALD IN HIS CHEST AGAINST THE WALL. "WHAT THE HELL ARE YOU DOING IN THERE? YOU'RE FUCKING UP OUR CASE"!

"YOU THINK I GIVE A DAMN ABOUT THIS CASE? I'M NOT GOING TO HELL FOR YOU OR DR.GOLDMAN", SAYS RUDY.

"WHAT ARE YOU TALKING ABOUT"?

"I'M TALKING ABOUT SAVING A LIFE! SHELTON HOLLOWAY IS A HUMAN BEING. I HOPE YOU ENJOY WHATEVER YOUR PAYOFF WAS! THAT WILL BE YOUR TICKET TO BURN IN HELL".

BACK IN COURTROOM

"WE'D LIKE TO CALLED SHERIFF PRICE TO THE WITNESS STAND", ANNOUNCES THE PROSECUTOR.

"SHERIFF, FOR THE RECORD, PLEASE STATE YOUR NAME AND OCCUPATION".

"JOHN PRICE, SHERIFF OF SUMTER COUNTY".

"I UNDERSTAND THAT YOU FIRST STARTED QUESTIONING SHELTON JEROME HOLLOWAY FOR THE MURDER OF PATRICIA HANNAH WHEN HE STARTED HANGING AROUND THE POLICE STATION".

"YES. INITIALLY, SHELTON HOLLOWAY WAS NOT A SUSPECT IN THIS CASE. HE TOLD ME

HE HAD OBSERVED SOMEONE ELSE ABDUCT PATRICIA HANNAH".

"HOW MANY TIMES DID YOUR DEPARTMENT QUESTION MR. HOLLOWAY"?

"MY DEPARTMENT QUESTIONED SHELTON HOLLOWAY FOUR TIMES ABOUT THE DEATH OF PATRICIA HANNAH. SHELTON HOLLOWAY WOULD OFTEN COME TO HEADQUARTERS WHEN WE HAD NO PLANS TO INTERVIEW HIM".

"FOR THE RECORD COULD YOU POINT OUT SHELTON JEROME HOLLOWAY".

SHERIFF PRICE POINTS. "HE'S RIGHT THERE".

"NO FURTHER QUESTIONS, YOUR HONOR".

"SHERIFF, YOU STATED MR. HOLLOWAY WOULD HANG AROUND EVEN IF YOU HAD NO PLANS TO QUESTION HIM", ASKS SHELTON'S ATTORNEY, MICHEAL RUSSO.

"THAT'S CORRECT".

"WHAT KILLER IN THEIR RIGHT FRAME OF MIND WOULD HAND AROUND A POLICE STATION IF THEY KILLED SOMEONE"?

"MR. HOLLOWAY".

"DID YOU READ MR. HOLLOWAY HIS MIRANDA RIGHT"?

"YES".

"DID HE UNDERSTAND HIS RIGHTS"?

"I BELIEVE SO".

"YOU BELIEVE SO"? HE WALK BACK TO GET HIS PAPERWORK. "ACCORDING TO THESE RECORDS, SHELTON JEROME HOLLOWAY WAS READ HIS RIGHTS, BUT TOLD DEPUTY WRIGHT HE DIDN'T KNOW WHAT MIRANDA RIGHTS WERE". HOLDING THE PAPER UP, "DOES THIS SOUND FAMILIAR, SHERIFF"?

"ACCORDING TO DEPUTY WRIGHT, SHELTON JEROME HOLLOWAY CLEARLY UNDERSTOOD HIS RIGHTS".

"SHERIFF ISN'T IT A FACT THAT SHELTON HOLLOWAY DID NOT UNDERSTAND HIS RIGHTS AND EVEN IF HE DID UNDERSTAND HIS RIGHTS HE DID NOT KNOWINGLY, INTELLIGENTLY, AND VOLUNTARILY WAIVE THEM"?

"THAT'S NOT TRUE"!

"ISN'T IT ALSO TRUE YOU ARE COVERING UP FOR THE REAL KILLER, WHO SURGICALLY REMOVED PATRICIA HANNAH'S EYES, LIVER, KIDNEY AND HEART"? HE TURNS AND LOOK AT DR. GOLDMAN.

"NOW WHY IN THE WORLD WOULD I DO THAT? I DON'T KNOW ABOUT ANY OF THAT".

"SHERIFF, I DON'T KNOW WHO YOU ARE COVERING UP FOR, BUT YOU GOT THE SHORT END OF THE STICK. WEALTHY CLIENTS PAY UP TO $150,000 FOR ORGANS. "I WONDER HOW MUCH YOU GOT".

JUDGE LEVY LOOKS AT COURT REPORTER. "THAT LAST STATEMENT WILL BE STRICKEN FROM THE RECORD".

"SORRY, YOUR HONOR. NO FURTHER QUESTIONS FOR THIS WITNESS".

SHERIFF PRICE WALKS OFF THE STAND AND GIVES DR. GOLDMAN A MEAN LOOK.

"WE'D LIKE TO CALL MABEL MAE HOLLOWAY TO THE WITNESS STAND", SAYS PROSECUTOR.

"FOR THE RECORD COULD YOU STATE YOU'RE NAME"?

"MABEL MAE HOLLOWAY", MRS. HOLLOWAY SAYS IN HER WHEELCHAIR.

"MRS. HOLLOWAY, ARE YOU THE MOTHER OF SHELTON JEROME HOLLOWAY AKA CHEESE"?

"YES".

"DID YOUR SON, SHELTON JEROME HOLLOWAY, KILL PATRICIA HANNAH"?

"YES, AROUND 3 A.M. ON APRIL 11TH, MY SON CAME HOME WITH BLOOD ON HIS SHIRT".

"DID HE SAY WHERE THE BLOOD COME FROM"?

"HE TOLD MY DAUGHTER THAT HE MADE A MISTAKE. THAT HE RAPED AND KILLED PATRICIA HANNAH".

DR. GOLDMAN SMILES.

"HE TOLD HIS SISTER THAT HE RAPED AND MURDERED PATRICIA HANNAH. NO FURTHER QUESTIONS YOUR HONOR".

"MRS. HOLLOWAY. WHAT LINE OF WORK ARE YOU IN", MR. RUSSO CROSS EXMAINES HER.

"OBJECTION YOUR HONOR WHAT DOES THAT HAVE TO DO WITH THIS CASE"?

"OVERRULED, CONTINUE".

"I DON'T WORK", WHISPERS MABEL HOLLOWAY.

"YOU DON'T WORK. IT IS TRUE THAT THE WELFARE DEPARTMENT CUT OFF YOUR FOOD STAMPS"?

"NO! HOW ELSE AM I GOING TO FEED MY FAMILY"?

"MRS. HOLLOWAY I HAVE A LETTER IN MY HAND FROM THE WELFARE DEPARTMENT STATING YOUR FOOD STAMPS WERE CUT OFF DUE TO YOUR ELIGIBILITY FOR CHILD SUPPORT".

"CHILD SUPPORT"?

"YES, CHILD SUPPORT. I BELIEVE THAT YOU TOLD SHERIFF PRICE YOUR SON, SHELTON HOLLOWAY, KILLED PATRICIA HANNAH SO YOU COULD COLLECT THE REWARD MONEY OF $20,000".

"I DON'T KNOW WHAT YOU'RE TALKING ABOUT"!

MICHAEL WALKS THE CHECK OVER TO MRS. HOLLOWAY. "IT STATES, I, MABEL HOLLOWAY, ACCEPT THIS CHECK FOR $20,000 AS A REWARD FOR ASSISTING IN IDENTIFYING THE SUSPECT IN THE MURDER OF PATRICIA ANN HOLLOWAY OF WARD, ALABAMA. IS THIS YOUR SIGNATURE ON THE BACK OF THIS CHECK"?

"YES".

"NO FURTHER QUESTIONS, YOUR HONOR".

JUDGE LEVY SHAKES HIS HEAD. "WE WILL STOP HERE. WE WILL CONTINUE THIS HEARING ON MONDAY OF NEXT WEEK".

CHAPTER 36

DR. GOLDMAN IS HAVING DINNER WITH PROSECUTOR STOKELY.

DR. GOLDMAN EATS HIS DINNER AND ASKS, "ARE WE GOING TO WIN THIS CASE"?

"THIS CASE WAS OVER BEFORE IT GOT STARTED, ANSWERS PROSECUTOR BLAKELY.

"GOOD", DR. GOLDMAN SAYS AS HE PASSES RICHARD STOKELY HIS CHECK. "JUST AS I PROMISED".

PROSECUTOR STOKELY LOOKS AT THE CHECK. "$50,000 WILL GET THE JOB DONE EVERYTIME"!

DEPUTY WRIGHT WALKS IN. "HERE'S THE CONFESSION TAPE SHERIFF PRICE REQUESTED".

PROSECUTOR RICHARD STOKELY LOOKS AT DR. GOLDMAN. "LIKE I SAID, THIS CASE WAS OVER

BEFORE IT GOT STARTED. DEPUTY, MAKE SURE THE TAPE HAS BEEN EDITED".

"I'LL TAKE THE TAPE WITH ME".

THE SHERIFF WALKS IN.

"GOOD TO SEE YOU AGAIN. IF YOU GENTLEMEN WILL EXCUSE ME, I HAVE BUSINESS TO DISCUSS WITH DR. GOLDMAN", SAYS SHERIFF PRICE.

PROSECUTOR, RICHARD STOKELY REPLIES, "CERTAINLY".

SHERIFF PRICE IS VISIBLY UPSET WITH DR. GOLDMAN. "WHY"?

"SHERIFF, I KNOW WHERE YOU'RE GOING WITH THIS. IT'S NOT TRUE WHAT RUSSO SAID IN COURT".

"REALLY"?

"WEALTHY CLIENTS DO PAY UP TO $150,000 PER ORGAN. BUT THIS CASE WAS DIFFERENT. MY DAUGHTER IN LAW NEEDED A HEART TRANS-PLANT. I FELT WHAT I PAID YOU WAS FAIR, CONSIDERING I HAVE BEEN MORE THAN GEN-EROUS WITH YOU IN THE PAST".

THE WAITRESS INTERRUPTS. "EXCUSE ME SHERIFF, CAN I GET YOU SOMETHING TO DRINK"?

"I'LL TAKE A GLASS OF WATER".

"ARE YOU DINING IN"?

"NO".

"SO YOU THINK IT WAS FAIR", ASKS SHERIFF PRICE.

"YES, IT WAS FAIR. YOU SAID IT YOURSELF. YOU HAVE ENOUGH MONEY TO BUY YOU A HOUSE IN DEMOPOLIS".

SHERIFF PRICE SMILES. "YEAH, YOU'RE RIGHT".

CHAPTER 37

SHELTON SITS IN THE SUMTER COUNTY JAIL.

"I CAN'T BELIEVE YOU WOULD DO THIS TO ME", SCREAMS SHELTON.

"SON, I DIDN'T HAVE A CHOICE! I HAD TO! MY FOOD STAMPS WERE CUT OFF, AND I TOLD YOU THAT I CAN'T GET CHILD SUPPORT", SAYS MRS. HOLLOWAY.

"WHAT MOTHER WOULD TURN HER SON IN FOR REWARD MONEY? YOU KNOW I DIDN'T KILLED PATRICIA".

"I KNOW SON. LOOK, YOU DON'T HAVE ANY-THING TO WORRY ABOUT. THE SYSTEM IS GO-ING TO FREE YOU. THERE'S NO EVIDENCE YOU KILLED PATRICIA HANNAH. AND THE JURY IS NOT GOING TO SEND SOMEBODY LIKE YOU TO PRISON".

"WHAT DO YOU MEAN, SOMEBODY LIKE ME"?

"YOU KNOW, SOMEBODY SLOW". MRS. HOL-LOWAY NOTICES THAT SHELTON IS HURT BY HER COMMENT, SO SHE CHANGES THE SUB-JECT QUICKLY. "THE SHERIFF WON'T LET THAT HAPPEN".

"I DON'T TRUST THE SHERIFF! HE AND DEPUTY WRIGHT MADE ME CONFESS TO THIS CRIME"!

"YOUR CONFESSION WON'T CONVICT YOU, SON. EVERYONE IN YORK KNOWS WHO KILLED PA-TRICIA. IT WAS THAT RACIST WHITE DOCTOR AND HIS SON! EVERYBODY IN YORK IS TALK-ING ABOUT THAT. IT WILL SOON GET RIGHT BACK TO THE SHERIFF, AND YOU WILL BE SET FREE".

CHAPTER 38

BACK IN SUMTER COUNTY COURTROOM

PROSECUTOR, RICHARD STOKELY SAYS, "YOUR HONOR, I'D LIKE TO CALL DR. MICHEAL BIVENS, CHIEF OF PSYCHIATRY AT TAYLOR UNITED MEDICAL FACILITY, TO THE WITNESS STAND".

"DR. BIVENS, DID YOU EVALUATE SHELTON JEROME HOLLOWAY AND PERFORM AN I.Q. TEST ON HIM"?

MICHEAL BIVENS REPLIES, "YES. SHELTON HOLLOWAY HAD A NUMBER OF TESTS THAT HAD PREVIOUSLY BEEN CONDUCTED PREVIOUSLY. HE RECEIVED AN I.Q. SCORE OF LESS THAN 40 WHEN HE WAS A CHILD. I CONDUCTED MY OWN TEST ON SHELTON HOLLOWAY AND DETERMINED HIS OVERALL I.Q. TO BE IN THE 60 TO 70 RANGE".

"OVERALL HIS I.Q. IS IN THE 60 TO 70 RANGE. MR. BIVENS DO YOU THINK MR SHELTON HOLLOWAY IS MENTALLY RETARDED"?

"NO, SHELTON HOLLOWAY IS BORDERLINE OR MILDLY SLOW. HE CLEARLY UNDERSTANDS THE DIFFERENCE BETWEEN RIGHT AND WRONG".

"FOR THE RECORD, WHERE DID YOU EVALUATE SHELTON JEROME HOLLOWAY"?

"AT THE TAYLOR UNITED MEDICAL FACILITY IN MERIDIAN, MISSISSIPPI".

"NO FURTHER QUESTIONS, YOUR HONOR".

MICHEAL RUSSO CROSS EXAMINES MR. BIVENS. "MR. BIVENS, MY MEDICAL EXPERT HERE IN TOWN TESTIFIED THAT MR. HOLLOWAY'S I.Q. IS STILL IN THE 40 RANGE. ARE YOU SURE THAT SOMEONE HASN'T INFLUENCED YOU TO SAY THAT MR. HOLLOWAY'S I.Q. IS HIGHER"?

MICHEAL BIVENS LAUGHS NERVOUSLY. "I DON'T KNOW WHAT YOU'RE TALKING ABOUT"!

MICHEAL RUSSO LAUGHS. "YOU DON'T KNOW WHAT I'M TALKING ABOUT? NOW YOU SAID THAT YOU CONDUCTED THE TEST IN MERIDIAN, MISSISSIPPI, BUT ISN'T IT TRUE THAT YOU CONDUCTED THE TEST IN SHERIFF PRICE'S OFFICE"?

"I DON'T KNOW WHERE YOU'RE GETTING YOUR INFORMATION! I CONDUCTED THE TEST IN MY OFFICE IN MERIDIAN"!

"YES, YOUR OFFICE IS LOCATED IN MERIDIAN, MISSISSIPPI, BUT YOU DIDN'T CONDUCT MR. HOLLOWAY'S I.Q. TEST THERE! YOU CONDUCTED SHELTON JEROME HOLLOWAY'S I.Q. TEST RIGHT HERE IN TOWN WITH YOUR FRIEND, SHERIFF PRICE"!

"MR. RUSSO, THAT'S NOT TRUE! YOU HAVE NO PROOF OF THAT"!

"NO FURTHER QUESTIONS, YOUR HONOR".

"WE WILL TAKE AN HOUR'S RECESS", SAYS THE JUDGE.

MICHEAL RUSSO WALKS THE HALL OUTSIDE THE COURTROOM.

PROSECUTOR RICHARD STOKELY AND SHERIFF PRICE IN THE HALL TALKING

SHERIFF PRICE LOOKS AT MICHEAL RUSSO. "YOU SELL OUT"!

"MICHAEL, YOU DON'T NEED THIS. THE KID IS POOR, BLACK AND MENTALLY RETARDED. WALK AWAY! HE'LL BE OUT IN TWENTY", SAYS THE PROSECUTOR.

"ARE YOU SCARED YOU'RE GOING TO LOSE THIS CASE", ASKS MICHEAL.

"NO CHANCE OF THAT HAPPENING! THIS IS STILL MY COURTROOM! DON'T YOU EVER FORGET THAT"!

BACK IN COURT

DEPUTY WRIGHT WHISPERS IN THE PROSECUTOR'S EAR. "YOUR HONOR, I WOULD LIKE TO REQUEST A DELAY IN THIS HEARING UNTIL TOMORROW. WE ARE STILL WAITING ON THE RESULTS ON THE POLYGRAPH TEST PERFORMED ON MR. HOLLOWAY. I NEED THOSE RESULTS FOR MY NEXT LINE OF QUESTIONING".

"WOULD YOU HAVE A PROBLEM WITH THAT MR. RUSSO"?

"NOT AT ALL, YOUR HONOR".

"THIS HEARING WILL CONTINUE TOMORROW MORNING AT 9AM".

PROSECUTOR RICHARD STOKELY WHISPERS IN SHERIFF'S EAR. "MEET ME IN MY OFFICE".

CHAPTER 39

"WE HAVE A PROBLEM, SHERIFF. WE HAVE WIT-NESSES, BUT NO EYE WITNESSES. AND THE CONFESSION TAPE IS DOUBTFUL AT BEST".

"DOUBTFUL".

PROSECUTOR, RICHARD STOKELY ANSWERS, "YES, DOUBTFUL".

DR. GOLDMAN WALKS IN.

"DON'T SHOW IT TO THE PUBLIC. JUST SHOW WHAT YOU NEED IN COURT", SAYS DR.GOLDMAN.

PROSECUTOR RICHARD STOKELY LOOKS SURPRISED.

"THAT'S RIGHT, IT'S BEEN EDITED ANYWAY. JUST USE WHAT YOU NEED TO MAKE YOUR CASE", SAYS SHERIFF PRICE.

CHAPTER 40

"ALL RISE. THE HONORABLE JUDGE LEVY PRESIDING".

"YOU MAY BE SEATED. MR. STOKELY, YESTERDAY YOU STATED THAT THE D.A. WAS WAITING FOR INFORMATION ON THE POLYGRAPH".

"YOUR HONOR, A POLYGRAPH WAS DONE AT THE SHERIFF'S DEPARTMENT HERE IN YORK IN JUNE, WHICH WAS INCONCLUSIVE. IN JULY, A SECOND POLYGRAPH WAS SCHEDULED. HOWEVER MR. HOLLOWAY SAID THAT THERE WAS NO POINT IN TAKING IT, BECAUSE HE WOULD NEVER PASS IT. HE STATED HE WOULD JUST LIKE TO TELL WHAT HAPPENED THE NIGHT THAT PATRICIA HANNAH DIED, ANSWERS PROSECUTOR STOKELY.

"DO YOU HAVE THAT EVIDENCE MR. STOKELY"?

"YES, YOUR HONOR, I DO".

"MR STOKELY, YOU MAY CALL YOUR NEXT WITNESS".

"I WOULD LIKE TO CALL MRS. HELEN HANNAH TO THE WITNESS STAND".

"MRS HANNAH, HE EMPTIES THE EVIDENCE FROM THE BROWN BAG, CAN YOU IDENTIFY THESE ITEMS"?

"MY DAUGHTER".

"WHAT WAS YOUR DAUGHTER'S NAME, MRS. HANNAH"?

"PATRICIA ANN HANNAH".

"CAN YOU IDENTIFY THESE BLUE JEANS"?

"THOSE WERE THE BLUE JEANS PATRICIA WORE TO THE DANCE".

"HOW CAN YOU BE SURE THAT THESE BLUE JEANS BELONG TO PATRICIA"?

"SHE TOLD ME THAT THOSE JEANS WERE HER FAVORITE PAIR BECAUSE I BOUGHT THEM FOR HER ON HER 16TH BIRTHDAY".

"WHEN MR. HOLLOWAY BROKE OUT OF JAIL, WHERE DID YOU SEE HIM"?

"DOWNTOWN".

"CAN YOU BE MORE SPECIFIC"?

"I SAW MR. HOLLOWAY WALKING DOWNTOWN YORK, ALABAMA".

"WAS HE HOLDING ANYTHING IN HIS HANDS WHEN YOU SAW HIM"?

"YES, HE WAS HOLDING A BROWN BAG".

"A BROWN BAG! MRS. HANNAH, HE HOLDS THE BROWN BAG UP, IS THIS THE BROWN BAG YOU SAW IN SHELTON HOLLOWAY'S HANDS"?

"YES", ANSWERS MRS. HANNAH.

"NO FURTHER QUESTIONS, YOUR HONOR".

"MR RUSSO, DO YOU WANT TO CROSS EXAMINE THE WITNESS"?

"YOUR HONOR, I HAVE NO QUESTIONS FOR MRS. HANNAH".

"YOUR HONOR, THE PROSECUTION RESTS ITS CASE".

"LET'S TAKE A HALF AN HOUR RECESS, AT WHICH TIME THE DEFENCE WILL COMMENCE ITS CASE".

"YOUR HONOR, I WOULD LIKE TO CALL MR. STEVEN JACKSON, AKA EDDIE LEE, TO THE WITNESS STAND".

"MR. JACKSON, FOR THOSE OF YOU WHO DON'T KNOW, STEVEN JACKSON GOES BY THE NAME EDDIE LEE, AND TO LAW OFFICIALS, IS KNOWN TO BE A PEEPING TOM. HE IS CURRENTLY SERVING A SIX MONTH SENTENCE IN JAIL FOR INDECENT EXPOSURE. MR. JACKSON, WHAT DID SHERIFF PRICE ASK YOU TO DO TO THE VICTIM'S MOTHER, MRS. HANNAH"?

"SHERIFF PRICE SAID IF I WANTED AN EARLY RELEASE FROM JAIL, I HAD TO CALL PATRICIA HANNAH'S MOTHER AND HARRASS HER".

"I'M HOLDING IN MY HAND EVIDENCE FROM TRACED CALLS FROM THE SUMTER COUNTY JAIL CELL TO MRS. HANNAH HOME. ACCORDING TO MY FILES, MR. STEVENS, IS IT TRUE YOU CALLED MRS. HANNAH HOUSE OVER TWENTY TIMES AND HUNG UP"?

"THAT'S CORRECT SIR", ANSWERS STEVEN.

"IS IT ALSO TRUE THAT SHERIFF PRICE TOLD YOU TO SAY THAT WHEN SHELTON HOLLO-WAY WAS FIRST PLACED BEHIND BARS THAT HE SAID, "GET THIS CAT OUT OT MY JAIL CELL BEFORE I KILL IT LIKE I DID PATRICIA ANN HANNAH, BECAUSE THERE WAS A CAT IN HIS CELL"?

"YES".

"NO FURTHER QUESTIONS, YOUR HONOR".

"MR STOKELY".

"I HAVE NO QUESTIONS FOR THIS WITNESS, YOUR HONOR".

"MR RUSSO, YOU MAY CALL YOUR NEXT WITNESS".

"YOUR HONOR, I'D LIKE TO CALL SHELTON JE-ROME HOLLOWAY TO THE WITNESS STAND".

SHELTON TAKES THE WITNESS STAND.

"MR. HOLLOWAY, DO YOU KNOW YOU'RE SCHOOL PRINCIPAL, MR. CARTER", ASKS MI-CHEAL RUSSO.

"YES", STUTTERS SHELTON.

"MR. HOLLOWAY, DID YOU ASSASSINATE MR. CARTER"?

"YES, I ASSASSINATE HIM EVERY TIME I SEE HIM", SMILES SHELTON.

"MR. HOLLOWAY, DID YOU ASSASSINATE YOUR TEACHER, MRS. JONES"?

"YES, I TRY TO ASSASSINATE ALL OF THE PEOPLE THAT I RESPECT".

"OBJECTION YOUR HONOR! WHAT DOES THIS HAVE TO DO WITH THIS CASE"?

"YOU'D BETTER EXPLAIN YOURSELF, MR. RUSSO", SAYS JUDGE LEVY.

"YOUR HONOR, THIS IS PROOF POSITIVE THAT MR. HOLLOWAY COULD NOT POSSIBLY UNDERSTAND HIS MIRANDA RIGHTS WHEN READ TO HIM BY THE OFFICER. AS FOR THE CONFESSION, HOW COULD HE POSSIBLY UNDERSTAND THE LINE OF QUESTIONING? HE DOESN'T HAVE COMMON SENSE! HE WAS WALKING DOWNTOWN WITH THE EVIDENCE IN A BROWN BAG! DOES THAT SEEM LOGICAL TO ANYONE IN THIS COURT".

"SUSTAINED, CONTINUE MR. RUSSO".

"MR. HOLLOWAY, DID YOU KILL PATRICIA HANNAH"?

"NO SIR"!

"WHAT ABOUT THE CONFESSION TAPE? DID YOU TELL SHERIFF PRICE AND DEPUTY WRIGHT THAT YOU KILLED PATRICIA HANNAH"?

"WELL YES, SIR! THEY MADE ME DO IT", STUTTERS SHELTON.

"HOW DID THEY DO THAT? CAN YOU TELL ME WHAT HAPPENED"?

"SHERIFF PRICE AND DEPUTY WRIGHT DROVE ME TO A NICE HOTEL IN MONTGOMERY, ALABAMA. WE WENT SHOPPING AND THEY BOUGHT ME A CHEESEBURGER AND SOME FRENCH FRIES".

"WAIT A MINUTE. SHERIFF CLAIMED YOU KILLED PATRICIA HANNAH IN YORK, ALABAMA. WHY WOULD HE DRIVE YOU 85 MILES OUT OF THE CITY"?

"THEY SAID THEY WANTED TO TAKE ME SOMEWHERE NICE. DID I TELL YOU THAT THEY BOUGHT ME A NICE NEW OUTFIT"?

"THEY BOUGHT YOU NEW CLOTHES TOO"?

"THEY SAID THEY WERE GOING TO GIVE ME SOME MONEY IF I CONFESS TO THE CRIME. I HAVEN'T SEEN THE MONEY YET, BUT THEY GAVE SOME MONEY TO MY MOMMA".

"NO FURTHER QUESTIONS YOUR HONOR".

"MR HOLLOWAY, CAN YOU PLEASE SPELL YOUR NAME"?

"SPELL MY NAME"?

"YES, SIR, SPELL YOUR NAME".

"S-H-E-L-T-O-N-H-O-L-L-O-W-A-Y".

"YOU SEE, SHELTON HOLLOWAY'S I.Q. ISN'T 40, IT'S 60! AND YES, HE DOES UNDERSTAND WHAT IS ASKED OF HIM! AND YES, HE UNDERSTOOD HIS MIRANDA RIGHTS! YOUR HONOR, I WOULD LIKE TO ENTER INTO EVIDENCE THE CONFESSION TAPE WHICH WILL SHOW THAT SHELTON HOLLOWAY DID IN FACT STATE THAT HE KILLED PATRICIA ANN HANNAH".

"LET'S SEE IT"!

PROSECUTOR, RICHARD STOKELY AND MICHEAL RUSSO WALK TO THE JURY STAND AND SHOW A FIVE SECOND CLIP OF SHELTON HOLLOWAY

CONFESSING TO THE CRIME.

"THAT'S NOT A CONFESSION! IT LOOKS LIKE SHERIFF PRICE AND DEPUTY WRIGHT MADE HIM SAY THAT! THAT TAPE HAS BEEN EDITED, EXPLAINS MICHEAL. "YOUR HONOR, CAN WE PLAY THE ENTIRE CONFESSION TAPE IN COURT"?

"NO! ARE WE READY FOR CLOSING ARGUMENTS"? BOTH MICHEAL AND PROSECUTOR STOKELY ANSWER YES.

"THERE WILL BE AN HOUR RECESS FOR LUNCH. WE'LL MEET BACK AT 2 P.M. TO HEAR CLOSING ARGUMENTS".

CHAPTER 41

PROSECUTOR RICHARD STOKELY IS ORDERING FOOD. HE IS STANDING IN LINE WAITING ON HIS ORDER. HE LOOKS BACK. "I TOLD YOU THIS CASE WAS OVER BEFORE IT GOT STARTED! YOU DIDN'T LISTEN TO ME"!

MICHEAL RUSSO SAYS, "YOU'VE LOST THIS CASE AND YOU KNOW IT"!

"LOST THE CASE? DID I HEAR YOU SAY I LOST THE CASE? MAYBE YOU'RE IN A DIFFERENT COURTROOM FROM THE REST OF US", THE PROSECUTOR LAUGHS.

"LET'S SEE. I UNDERSTAND THAT A CERTAIN DR. GOLDMAN PAID YOU, THE SHERIFF, THE JUDGE AND PROBABLY THE JURY OFF".

"DR. GOLDMAN IS A GOOD, UPSTANDING CITIZEN OF THIS COMMUNITY"!

"IT'S AMAZING WHAT MONEY CAN MAKE SOME PEOPLE DO".

"MAYBE THE NEXT TIME YOU WOULD CHOOSE TO REPRESENT A CLIENT WHO'S WEALTHY".

"MY CLIENT MAY BE POOR, BUT HE IS INNOCENT AND YOU KNOW IT"!

"INNOCENT TO YOU, BUT FOR THE RECORD, HE'S GOING DOWN AS GUILTY TODAY, SNEERS THE PROSECUTOR.

"ORDER NUMBER 62".

"THAT'S MY ORDER, GOTTA GO".

CHAPTER 42

CLOSING ARGUMENTS FOR PROSECUTOR IS UNDERWAY.

"THE MOST IMPORTANT FACTOR IN THIS CASE IS THE CONFESSION TAPE. SHELTON HOLLOWAY WASN'T MENTALLY RETARDED, HE WAS STREET SMART. HE WAS ABOUT TO GRADUATE FROM SUMTER COUNTY HIGH SCHOOL. HE WAS HOLDING DOWN TWO JOBS. THAT DOESN'T SOUND LIKE SOMEONE WITH MENTAL PROBLEMS, DOES IT"?

"ON THE NIGHT OF APRIL 11TH, SHELTON HOLLOWAY SAW PATRICIA HANNAH AT THE DANCE. SHELTON HOLLOWAY WANTED A SEXUAL RELATIONSHIP WITH PATRICIA HANNAH, BUT SHE ALREADY WAS IN A COMMITTED RELATIONSHIP WITH SOMEONE ELSE. HE GOT MAD AND DECIDED TO KILL HER"!

"LADIES AND GENTLEMEN OF THE JURY, I STAND BEFORE YOU TODAY TO SAY THAT SHELTON

JEROME HOLLOWAY AKA CHEESE IS THE PERSON WHO COMMITTED THIS CRIME! I PLEAD WITH YOU TO FIND HIM GUILTY AND TAKE THIS DANGEROUS MAN OFF THE STREETS OF OUR PEACEFUL TOWN. THANK YOU"!

MICHEAL RUSSO'S CLOSING ARGUMENT

"IT IS SAID THAT MANY PEOPLE WITH RETARDATION SMILE A LOT. YOU HAVE HEARD TESTIMONY FROM MANY CITIZENS OF YORK, WHO ALL AGREE THAT SHELTON IS A HARMLESS INDIVIDUAL, WHO WOULDN'T HURT A FLY. WHEN THE SHERIFF'S DEPARTMENT SAW HIS SMILING FACE COMING, THEY KNEW THAT THEY HAD FOUND SOMEONE ON WHOM TO PIN THIS MURDER. PRIOR TO THIS, THEY HAD NOTHING! HIS MOTHER TELLS THE SHERIFF THAT HE CONFESSED TO THE CRIME, BUT SHE ALSO LIED TO THE STATE IN ORDER TO GET ASSISTANCE. SO ARE WE TO BELIEVE HER"?

"HOW CAN SHELTON JEROME HOLLOWAY SURGICALLY REMOVE PATRICIA ANN HANNAH'S ORGANS WHEN HE'S NOT SKILLED ENOUGH TO TAKE A KNIFE AND OPEN A CAN OF TUNA? SOMEONE WITH SKILL KILLED PATRICIA HANNAH. AND WHERE IS THE SPERM EVIDENCE LINKING MR. HOLLOWAY TO THIS CRIME? THERE IS NONE! SO WHERE DOES THE

RAPE ACCUSATION EVEN ENTER INTO THESE PROCEEDINGS"?

"IT IS THERFORE MY BELIEF THAT SHELTON JE-ROME HOLLOWAY IS INNOCENT, INNOCENT, INNOCENT"!

CHAPTER 43

AT THE GOLDMAN HOME, MRS. GOLDMAN IS QUESTIONING HER SON ABOUT HIS INVOLVEMENT IN THE MURDER.

"SON, DID YOU KILL THAT GIRL PATRICIA HANNAH"?

DAVID'S BACK IS TURNED. "MOM, IT WAS AN ACCIDENT. I JUST WANTED TO SLEEP WITH HER, BUT SHE KEPT ON CRYING, SO I DID IT ANYWAY. SHE KEPT SCREAMING, SO I GRABBED HER AROUND THE NECK TO SHUT HER UP. I MUST HAVE SQUEEZED TOO HARD, BECAUSE SHE STOPPED BREATHING. DAD TOLD ME TO TAKE HER TO HIS OFFICE. I DON'T KNOW WHAT HE DID WITH HER AFTER THAT".

CHAPTER 44

"WE THE JURY, FIND THE DEFENDANT SHEL-
TON JEROME HOLLOWAY GUILTY OF MURDER
IN THE FIRST DEGREE AND OF SEXUAL AS-
SAULT AS A LESSER OFFENSE INCLUDED IN THE
CAPITAL MURDER VERDICT".

SHELTON HOLLOWAY SMILES AND WAVES AT
THE JURY FOREMAN

CHAPTER 45

EPILOGUE

JEROME HOLLOWAY IS CURRENTLY SERVING A
LIFE SENTENCE, WITHOUT THE POSSIBILITY
OF PAROLE, AT STATON CORRECTIONAL FACIL-
ITY IN ALABAMA. HE HAS LOST EVERY APPEAL
THAT HE HAS HAD TO DATE.